UNTIL NOW

DELANEY DIAMOND

GARDEN AVENUE PRESS

Spanish Translations

Acere – Cuban slang meaning bro, dude, buddy

Cabrón – Bastard, jackass

Ahí está! – There it is!

¡Ganamos! – We won!

Hasta la proxima – See you next time, Until next time

Lo siento – I'm sorry

Mierda - Shit

¿Que bola? – Cuban slang meaning How's it going? or What's up?

1

Cruz Cordoba swam quietly along the edge of the pier and then slipped from the dark water, army-crawling up the grass toward the mansion with a pair of night-vision goggles over his eyes that cast a greenish glow on his surroundings. He flipped the goggles on top of his head and assessed the landscape. Crouching in the shadows in a black wetsuit, he'd be hard to see.

There were three guards in his line of sight—two smoking and talking near the back door, another slowly walking the length of the second-floor balcony that ran along the back side of the house. All three were well-dressed with no visible weapons, but he recognized the gun bulge at their hips beneath those tailored suits.

Through the floor-to-ceiling window to the left side of the house, guests milled around in floor-length gowns and tuxedos, sipping champagne and laughing as if they didn't have a care in the world. They had no idea the man their political party had nominated to represent the state of Maine was a lover of snuff films—that *he* starred in.

Of course, there was also the money-laundering and

rumors of using shell corporations to give donations to anti-government domestic terrorist groups, none of which had derailed his political career. Everyone knew he had presidential aspirations, but maybe a murder charge would finally do the trick before the piece of shit took down the whole country.

Cruz checked his watch and set the timer so it started counting down from ten. Ten minutes max to get in, retrieve the video, and get out. The delivery to a local journalist would take place in another location.

He eased to the edge of the brush and stayed low, waiting for the right moment. It was easier to take the men one at a time, but he'd tackle them both at once if he had to.

He removed the KA-BAR knife from his hip, blade facing backward as he gripped the handle and waited. As luck would have it, one of the men stubbed out his cigarette and sauntered back inside, while the other—a blond—remained behind to finish his cigarette. The one at the top was on his way down to the other end of the balcony, so when the blond turned his back to walk the length of the building, Cruz bolted across the grass.

Stealthy as a cat in his bare feet, he grabbed him from behind and slit his throat before he could scream. Nothing but the sound of a low gurgle escaped as Cruz supported him until he crumbled to the ground.

He wiped the blade on his thigh to get rid of the blood and paused, ears cocked as he listened. No unusual sounds, so he was on the go again, moving swiftly in the opposite direction away from the window that exposed the partying guests. The agency had planted a waitress with the caterers, and if she did her part right, there should be an open window on the ground floor for him to crawl through.

Cruz stopped at the window and tugged up, and it gave easily. He pushed it higher and slipped in, then eased it back down. Once again, he paused and listened, which gave his eyes time to adjust to the dark interior. The sitting room was filled with antique chairs and portraits on the walls and smelled stuffy, as if it wasn't used often.

He'd memorized the floorplan of the house and knew exactly where to go. He tiptoed across the carpet and cracked open the door. No movement in the hallway, but he could hear the distant chatter of the guests and the music playing from the live band.

The office was at the end of the hall. He eased out and moved quietly as he approached the heavy oak door. He tried the knob and it turned.

Perfect.

This was almost too easy. A quick glance behind him showed the hallway was still empty, so he let himself into the room.

With a quick glance at his watch, he saw four minutes down, six to go.

He lifted the oil painting of the White House off the wall and, placing it on the floor, exposed the safe. He'd already memorized the combination, so he turned the dial according to the numbers and tugged open the door.

Cruz couldn't suppress a smile. Now for the treasure inside. He found the video easy enough—an old VHS tape sitting atop a stack of papers. Might as well take the papers, too. Who knew what nuggets of additional information could be found on those pages. He stuffed everything into the waterproof bag he lifted from inside his wetsuit, stuck it back in the suit and zipped up the front. That's when he heard the door open.

"Don't move," a gravelly voice warned.

Dammit.

Cruz listened to the faint sound of footsteps coming toward him on the soft carpet.

"Who the hell are you!" the man demanded in a loud voice.

Worried that his raised voice would invite other guards to

come investigate, Cruz decided to defuse the situation by calmly asking, "Can I turn around?" He slowly lifted his hands to show he didn't have a weapon.

"Take. Your. Time," the man warned.

Cruz heard the safety disengage from the gun and did just that—took his time—not wanting to make any sudden moves that could cause his trigger-happy opponent to shoot—accidentally or on purpose.

He turned and found himself face to face with the guard who'd stubbed out his cigarette. Dark-haired, he was about an inch taller than Cruz but not as wide, with a scowling face and shaved head.

"Who the fuck are you?" the man asked.

"Pablo didn't tell you I was coming?" He needed to buy time, and bluffing helped him do that.

Right away, he guessed one thing about the man—he didn't want to pull the trigger. The gunshot would be heard by the guests and questions would be asked. Which meant he'd try to detain Cruz and find out what the hell he was doing there. All of which worked in Cruz's favor.

The guy frowned. "Pablo who?"

Not too bright, this one.

"You know Pablo. He works for Senator Peaslee."

"There ain't no Pablo." Finally, he was catching on.

"Maybe I'm in the wrong place then. I should leave."

His attempt at humor didn't go over well. "No way." The guy scowled and moved closer, holding his hand straight out and pointing the gun at the middle of Cruz's chest.

Now he was in the perfect position for Cruz to disarm him. Attempting to grab someone else's weapon was always a risky proposition, but he'd done it plenty of times. Wise men knew to remain at least a few feet out of reach so that if the victim moved quickly, you'd have time to fire off a round. Foolishly, the guard was standing too close.

Distract.

Grab.

Kill.

"You want to talk to Senator Peaslee about it? Go ahead, call him," Cruz said, hands still raised in fake surrender.

As the guard hesitated, Cruz snapped the fingers of his left hand. That caused the other man's eyes to shift toward the noise. Within that split second, Cruz snatched the gun and stepped out of reach.

The guard's eyes widened, and he thrust his hands in the air.

"Never hesitate." Cruz pulled the trigger.

The bullet hit the middle of his forehead as the sound blasted through the room. The man's head tipped backward, and he crashed to the floor.

Four minutes left.

He tossed the gun to the desk and dragged one of the guest chairs under the doorknob. That should slow down anyone coming to investigate the noise.

He closed the safe and replaced the painting. Hopefully they wouldn't guess he'd accessed the safe and removed the video, thus taking them by surprise. Since he couldn't go back the way he came, he lifted a window and swung onto the grass.

"Hey!" a voice yelled.

Two men in suits raced toward him. Cruz sprinted away from them, his long legs eating up the earth. The sound of handgun bullets cracked in the air. Clearly, they were no longer worried about disturbing the guests.

Several rounds whizzed way too close to his ear as he dodged and ducked in the dark, weaving a crooked line toward the water.

More voices yelling. There must be at least four of them now.

Taking a deep breath, he dived into the bay and sank to the

shallow bottom, curling into the smallest ball his body could contort into as he pressed his back against the embankment. Bullets rained into the water from above, but he kept still. Depending on angle and velocity, the bullets could penetrate the water up to seven feet, so he didn't want to move and risk getting shot.

He could hold his breath for six minutes but didn't have that much time. He had three minutes tops to get out of there if he wanted to make the rendezvous location in time.

The men argued. Cruz remained still.

One minute. The voices moved farther away.

Two minutes. No more sounds. To be sure they were gone, he stayed put.

Three minutes.

Now he'd take a chance.

Cruz resurfaced under the pier and pulled air into his lungs. Above, through the cracks in the wood, he saw a man standing guard on the shore. Dragging the goggles over his eyes, he took another deep breath and dived into the bay, swimming underwater for a few minutes before returning to the surface.

With long, steady strokes, he moved swiftly toward the rendezvous point—a boat that awaited him on the water. Pretty soon the senator's men would come looking for him in their boats, and he wanted to be far away by the time they did.

2

Cruz slammed down his domino and pumped his fist in the air. "Domino! *¡Ganamos!*"

He high-fived his partner, an older Cuban man with dark brown skin and salt-and-pepper hair who'd talked so much trash Cruz had been worried they'd have to eat crow at the end of the game. The other two Cubans they beat grumbled in Spanish and shook their heads.

"How much do I owe you?" Mr. Dominguez asked in Spanish.

"Nothing. I won't take your money, but I will take this." Cruz lifted the Panama hat from the older man's head and dropped it atop his own. "Perfect fit," he said with a grin, popping an unlit cigar into his mouth.

Whenever he was in the mood for a game of dominoes, he swung by Domino Park on Calle Ocho. This was where the old heads played and had been playing for decades. The air was filled with the scent of cigar smoke and the sound of Spanish as the men argued and laughed during the lively competition at multiple tables.

Mr. Dominguez scowled at him. Laughing, Cruz stood, making ready to leave.

"You can't go now. Give me a chance to win my hat back," Mr. Dominguez said.

"Another time, *señor*. *Hasta la proxima*." Cruz tipped his newly won hat at the three men and sauntered away.

"*Cabrón*," he heard one of them mutter.

He chuckled to himself.

Dominguez's daughter walked toward him, sizing him up with her eyes. "*Oye, Cruz. ¿Que bola?*" She swung her head to look at him as she passed by.

He turned to look at her, too, and was tempted to engage her in conversation but changed his mind, instead shooting her a grin and simply answering, "*Estoy bien*."

She was the kind who wanted a relationship, and he was nowhere ready for one. In his line of work, he couldn't offer her anything permanent, anything real. And keeping his distance meant Dominguez wouldn't try to shoot him on sight for messing with his daughter.

Cruz hopped into his '84 Cadillac El Dorado and gunned the engine. The car hadn't been much to look at when he bought her, but after a new engine and a paint job that covered it in pristine white paint, she looked as good as new and easily accommodated a man of his size. What he liked best was on a day like today, with the sun shining and the weather balmy, the long drive to Islamorada in the Florida Keys could be enjoyed with the top down.

Donning sunglasses, he cranked up the music and took off. An hour and a half later, he pulled into his favorite beachside bar, Tiki Grill. As soon as Cruz stepped out of the car, another vehicle pulled in behind him. The black sedan parked in an empty space and a man exited from the back. This man was an unwelcome sight.

"Miles," he muttered.

Miles Garrison was his contact at Plan B, the government agency he started working for twelve years ago, at the young age of eighteen. Plan B had no records and no budget. Officially, they didn't exist but operated under the concept that America's greatest threats come from within her borders. Greed, prejudice, and hate breed these problems, and a special team was needed to control the fallout when all else failed. Very few knew who they were. Some were assassins, others were spooks, and still others—like Cruz—a combination of the two.

The fact that Miles had shown up in person couldn't be good. His visit not only meant Cruz's vacation was about to end, it meant his next assignment was major.

A tall Black man with short-cropped hair and a full beard, Miles was completely overdressed in a three-piece suit and tie and carrying a briefcase.

"How's it going?" he asked.

"Better when you weren't here," Cruz replied, heading toward his favorite table near the water.

Miles chuckled, taking the dismissal in stride. "I need to talk to you."

"Who's in the car?"

"That's what I need to talk to you about."

Cruz glanced over his shoulder. Miles was no longer smiling.

In the open-air restaurant, they walked to a table that overlooked the Gulf. It was mid-afternoon, with only a few patrons and a skeleton crew of staff at work.

Cruz sat with his back to the wall and held up two fingers to the bartender, who nodded his understanding.

"I hate to bother you since you just came back from that assignment in Maine, but this couldn't wait. Good job with Senator Peaslee, by the way."

The senator had been placed under arrest once the news hit

the papers and the airwaves. His whole house of cards was tumbling down—as it should be.

"What are you doing here? I thought you never left your cushy office in DC. Since when do they send you on errands?"

The bartender arrived with two chilled bottles of Corona.

"Thanks," Cruz said.

"Since I'm on my way to the Virgin Islands on a family vacation, I offered to stop by and meet with you."

"Bullshit."

Miles's lips twisted into a slight smile. "Okay, fine. I was instructed to meet with you. I have a high-priority assignment that's off the books."

This wasn't an unusual request, since his services had been "loaned" out before to the governments of other countries. "Which country?"

"Not a country, a person. The person who wants to hire your services is Karen Sandoval, niece of Senator Joseph Sandoval from Texas."

Cruz's eyebrows shifted higher. Joseph Sandoval was a wealthy businessman and long-serving politician on The Hill. He was currently chairman of the Senate Committee on Appropriations, one of the most powerful committees in the Senate.

"You have my attention," he said, taking a swig of beer.

"Ms. Sandoval believes her estranged husband was murdered, and she wants us to help her prove it."

"Sounds like a job for law enforcement," Cruz said.

"One of the higher ups offered your services because she wants the best, and that's you. The murder took place in Houston, but they have a lead in Miami. You're familiar with the city, so..."

"Who's paying? I don't work for free." Cruz tipped the bottle to his lips and took another sip. Since this was a private deal, he needed to understand right away who was paying and when, particularly since the lines of this assignment seemed blurry at best.

"You'll get your usual freelance fee, half upfront and the other half when the job is done."

Cruz shrugged. "Fine. I'll listen."

"Good." Miles pulled a phone from his jacket pocket and lifted it to his ear. "Send her in."

Miles went to the door and came back with Karen Sandoval. She approached, looking poised and elegant and wearing a simple navy dress with a string of pearls around her neck. Her dark brown hair was going gray and was worn in a layered, textured style that spilled onto her shoulders.

"Hello, Mr...?"

"No need for names. How can I help you?"

"Okay." She smiled faintly. "Thank you for seeing me and for taking this job."

"I haven't taken it yet."

Miles glared at him.

"Oh." Karen glanced at Miles, who nodded for her to proceed. "Do you mind if I sit down?"

"Please, have a seat." Cruz motioned to one of the empty chairs at the round table. "Would you like something to drink?"

"Water would be nice."

Karen sat down, and Cruz called out the order for a water. The bartender came over right away and set it down beside her. Seated across from her and Miles, Cruz relaxed and waited.

Karen took a sip of water and cleared her throat. "I'll pay whatever you need me to, because I need to find out who killed my...estranged husband and why. My husband's name is Dennis Ray. He was an investigative reporter for the *Houston Times*, an old and well-respected newspaper. He ended up in jail, accused of using drugs and stealing data in the course of his investigation. No one will tell me what this data was because they claim it's a matter of national security. I was also told that he committed suicide. I'm not sure I believe that. I'm not sure I believe any of it. He's not a thief and he wouldn't kill himself."

"That doesn't mean he didn't," Cruz said.

"I'm convinced I'm right, on both counts," she insisted, her voice firmer.

Cruz flicked his gaze to Miles, whose expression remained emotionless. Returning his attention to Karen, he said, "Forgive me for asking, but how did the two of you end up together?"

That faint smile again. "We met at a coffee shop. He accidentally picked up my order and we had a good laugh about it. The next thing I knew, I was giving him my phone number. My father passed away some years ago, and my uncle became a surrogate father to me. He didn't approve of Dennis, and when I told him we were getting married, he said I was making a mistake. He didn't think Dennis was good enough for me and because Dennis is—was—fifteen years younger than I am, thought he was after my money. He wanted me to marry someone in politics, someone with connections. But Dennis was charming and funny, and I didn't care that he didn't have money. I had enough for the two of us. I fell in love with him.

"But money became a big issue for us—more for Dennis than me, really. When I had our daughter, Emily, he became distant, withdrawn. He complained that he didn't fit in at any of our social events, and...well, after a while, he stopped attending functions with me altogether, claiming that he had to work. We grew further apart. Money became a constant bone of contention between us, and I finally asked him for a divorce."

Pain flickered across her face as she stared down at her hands and played with the wedding rings on her finger.

She lifted her gaze and continued. "After a while, Dennis started talking about a reconciliation, but I didn't think it was a good idea. We were so different, and for six years we hadn't been able to make our marriage work." Her expression became earnest. "One day he told me that he was working on something big—an exposé that was lifechanging. He said he'd noticed a pattern in some data that he'd collected, but every time I asked him about the details, he dodged the questions. I didn't believe him, but he was so insistent, I started to wonder. I hired a private investigator to follow him. That's when I found out about...the other woman." She swallowed.

Miles opened his briefcase and removed a mini-computer that looked like a silver portable DVD player. He pressed his thumb to the biometric panel on top and it snapped open. He shoved it across the table to Cruz.

The dark screen lit up and populated with a series of photos, and Cruz flipped through them. The first few were of buildings, but he stopped when he came to the photo of a woman. He was immediately captivated by one of the most beautiful women he had ever seen.

She had golden skin and laughing brown eyes and was thick bodied with a round face. In the photo, she wore an off-the-shoulder, loose-fitting dress covered in a gold and blue geometric design, and her pink lips were puckered toward the person holding the camera. In another photo, she was standing with a flower in her hand. The picture looked like it could have been pulled from her Instagram account, with its perfect lighting and the way the sun reflected off her curly black hair.

"The few days my investigator followed him, Dennis spent a lot of time with the woman in the photos. One night he slept over at her apartment."

"What's her name?" Cruz asked.

"Shanice Lawrence. She left Texas three days after he died, and we lost track of her for a while but found her in Miami a few days ago. If anyone knows why he was killed, I believe she does, and if she had anything to do with it, I want her punished to the fullest extent of the law."

Cruz tore his gaze from the beguiling woman in the photos. "They officially ruled his death a suicide?"

Miles spoke up. "The official conclusion was suicide by hanging."

"What's the unofficial conclusion?" Cruz asked.

Miles glanced at Karen from the corner of his eye before answering in a grave voice, "We believe he was tortured to death."

Karen winced and closed her eyes.

Cruz shook his head in disgust. Torture should always be a last resort. For one, it didn't always yield the answers people wanted, and then there were results like this, where the torturer went too far and the interrogation ended in a mess.

There were better ways to get information out of people. Fear and intimidation worked in a pinch because a prisoner in a bad situation did *not* want the situation to get worse. Cruz's favorite method was to get the mark to trust him. It was a delicate dance and took time, but if done right, yielded the best results.

"Any idea what he was investigating?"

Miles nodded at Karen to continue.

"No, but for every major assignment he worked on, he kept a separate notebook. There must be a notebook somewhere that contains the data he had collected, which might help us understand why he was killed. From the little bit of information he gave me, I believe he uncovered something that could get someone in a lot of trouble, and they were desperate to get their hands on that evidence. After Dennis died, my house and car were broken into and ransacked, and I believe they were searching for that information. After what happened to him, and with a child to protect, I moved to my uncle's ranch in south Texas. I feel safer now, but I need to find that information because I believe it's the key to understanding why Dennis was killed. Will you help me?"

Cruz tapped his finger on the table. "I need to speak to Miles privately," he said.

Karen appeared flustered. As the niece of a powerful and prominent senator, she was probably used to people doing as she asked and had expected an answer.

"All right." She stood and looked at him with pleading eyes. "You know who I am, but I haven't told my uncle that I was meeting with you. *I* will pay your fee, whatever that is."

Cruz waited while Miles walked her out.

When he returned and sat down, Miles said, "Well? What's your answer?"

He crossed his arms over his chest. "Do you think anyone else knows about the mistress?"

"Maybe, maybe not. She's still alive, which means she knows nothing, or they haven't found her yet. A few things I did learn, she never visited Dennis in jail, and she has a unique setup where she works in Miami. She works at a bookstore named The Bookish Attic, and the owner pays her under the table and rented her a room in her house. They live about ten minutes from the shop. Everything you need is in the file. We need you to get close to her and find out what she knows, and if she has that notebook. If she has it, we need you to get it."

"A notebook? Are you shitting me?"

Miles shrugged. "I'm not judging anyone's method of record-keeping."

Cruz grunted and rubbed the back of his neck.

"Cruz, this is a simple job and easy money."

"Nothing is ever simple."

"This one should be. All you have to do is get the data. Whatever information Dennis gathered or stole, the mistress probably knows about it. Why else would she leave town so quickly?"

Cruz's gaze was drawn to the screen again—the woman's eyes, her smile. He scrolled through some more photos, admiring the way Shanice's ample curves filled out her outfits, showing off a full bosom, generous hips, and thick thighs. He didn't condone cheating, but he understood why Dennis had strayed. This was a sexy woman with a great ass.

"What about the national security angle? You believe that?" he asked.

Miles shrugged. "Hard to say."

Cruz tapped his thumb on the surface of the table. Finally, he asked, "When do I start?"

Miles let out a sigh of relief. "Tomorrow. Your ID, a wardrobe, et cetera—everything you need for your cover—are waiting at the apartment we're getting ready for you. Your name is Vicente Diaz, and you're an accountant."

"An accountant?" Cruz dragged his eyes from the screen and one of the surveillance photos showing Shanice at the grocery store examining a container of eggs.

"The investigator found an old profile for Shanice on one of those dating sites. She likes poetry and history. I think something low-key would be appropriate in this case."

Interesting. Cruz enjoyed history and poetry, as well. He believed history was the key to understanding societal norms and firmly agreed with philosopher George Santayana's famous quote: *Those who cannot remember the past are condemned to repeat it.* Though he didn't read a lot of poetry anymore, he appreciated the art form. His grandmother used to read poems to him as a kid. Her favorite poets included Cuban greats José Martí and Nicolás Guillén.

"What do I do if there are any...problems?"

"Do whatever you need to do," Miles said gravely.

No one enjoyed killing, but sometimes it had to be done. Cruz had become immune to the emotional toll that would affect someone less seasoned in his line of work. In his profession, emotions were more than a nuisance. They could derail a mission and get him killed.

"And the woman, Shanice?" he asked, his stomach tightening unexpectedly.

"Whatever you need to do," Miles repeated, his expression not wavering.

Cruz nodded. "Have Ms. Sandoval deposit that first payment in my account, and I'll be in touch when it's done."

3

"There he is."

Shanice tried not to look up when Ava made her comment in a hushed voice, but it was impossible not to.

She glanced up and saw *him,* walking toward the back of the bookstore. For the past week, he'd come in almost every night around the same time, an hour before the store closed at seven. He took his time browsing the shelves before coming to the front with his selections.

He was a mountain of a man. At five-nine, she often wore flats so she wouldn't be taller than her dates, but she wouldn't have to worry about that with this guy. She could wear heels and he'd still be taller by almost six inches. He had to be at least six foot five with a powerful build and wore glasses perched on a crooked nose that looked like it had been broken a few times. Long sleeves hid obviously muscular arms, and he was handsome in a rough, textured kind of way, exuding a quiet strength that intrigued her.

"Phew, he's fine," Ava whispered, fanning herself with a

magazine that caused her wispy blonde hair to blow back from her face.

Although Shanice hadn't worked at The Bookish Attic for long, Ava had been there for three years. Once Shanice started, they became friends. Ava had a good sense of humor and a great personality that meshed perfectly with Shanice's. Both women were always glad when they were scheduled at the same time because they got along extremely well.

Despite liking Ava, Shanice didn't share everything with her. She never told her about Dennis's death and why she'd moved to Florida from Texas. Guilt still ravaged her when she imagined Dennis hanging in that cell, though she'd never actually seen him in that condition. Could she have done more to help him?

"I can't argue with your assessment," Shanice said, eyes following their customer as he browsed the poetry shelves. Pleated pants fit snug on his tight behind, and the dress shirt pulled a little across his broad back.

"I would wear him out if he ever gave me the chance," Ava murmured.

Shanice used her ample hips to bump her skinny friend. "Stop. He'll hear you," she whispered.

"Wouldn't that be nice." Ava leaned closer. "Why don't you make a move on him and stop drooling in silence? Do it, or I will, and I won't hesitate to tell you all about it."

Both women snickered and went back to taking care of the end-of-evening tasks. Shanice straightened the area behind the cash register and prepped for when their eye-catching guest came to the front to check out. Right now, he was one of only three customers in the store, and it was quiet, making this the perfect time to start closing up shop.

Fifteen minutes before closing, the last two customers were gone and Ava went onto the sales floor to straighten up and reshelve stray books. Like clockwork, five minutes before they locked the doors, their favorite patron came forward with a thick hardcover book in hand. Shanice smiled, meeting his gaze head-on, heart racing way too fast over a man she barely knew, except for the fact that he seemed to like history and had a sexy, crooked smile. He also made her panties wet. She'd had way too many fantasies about loosening his tie and straddling his lap while she took full advantage of those succulent-looking lips.

"Found everything you're looking for?" she asked.

"I think so." He shoved the horn-rimmed glasses higher on his nose. "You've really expanded your poetry selection."

His voice carried the accented sound of Spanish pronunciation, and she wondered about his background.

"You noticed," she said, ridiculously pleased by his observation. "Our buyer tries to have a good selection for our customers."

"Well, I can assure you, it's greatly appreciated." He set a history tome of about six hundred pages on the counter and pulled a wallet from his back pocket. "I ordered a copy of *The Federalist Papers* the first time I came in, and I received a call that it has arrived."

"Okay. What was your last name again? Diaz, right?"

As if she needed to ask. She had memorized his name and phone number from that very day when he placed the order. By the second time he'd come in and purchased a book, she'd memorized his credit card digits.

"That's right."

Shanice rubbed sweaty hands down her hips.

His eyes, the color of a deep, dark umber, flicked over the movement before coming back to her face. Air trapped in her throat and tension tightened in the space between them.

"One moment," she whispered, because just like that, she'd lost her voice. She turned away and briefly closed her eyes.

Pretending to search the shelves though she knew exactly

where his book was located, she allowed herself a few seconds to regroup.

"Here we go," she said, holding up the book.

She handed it to him and he turned it over in his hand, as if admiring a piece of fine art. He had large hands with long, thick fingers. "*Bueno.*"

She lived for the sound of his voice, with its Spanish lilt, but delighted even more when he said a word or two in his native tongue.

Shanice rang up the two purchases and swiped the card.

She handed over the receipt, and after he'd signed his name, she bagged the books in one of their plastic sacks.

"Thank you very much, Mr. Diaz."

"Please, call me Vicente."

She blushed. "Vicente."

"You work a lot. Every time I come in, you're behind this counter."

"I don't mind. It's not really work when you love what you do," Shanice said. Feeling a surge of boldness, she added, "Where are you from?"

"Ah, the accent, eh? I haven't been able to shake it, no matter how hard I try." He shook his head as if disappointed.

"You shouldn't try to lose it. It's....nice."

"Thank you. I'm from Cuba—Havana, to be exact."

"How long have you lived here?"

"About fourteen years now. How about you—have you lived in Miami long?"

"Not long. I moved here from Texas a couple of months ago."

"Why here?"

She paused, unsure how to answer. She definitely couldn't tell the truth. "I, uh, needed a change. I have family outside of Houston, but my mother moved back to Arizona, where she's from, and my father died a few years ago. There didn't seem to be much reason to stick around, and Miami is beautiful. Great people, beautiful beaches—I may never leave."

"I'm sorry to hear about your father."

"I'm better now." Shanice played with a pen on the counter. "Um, what kind of work do you do?"

He winced. "Nothing interesting. I'm a boring forensic accountant."

"Sounds interesting to me. How is forensic accounting different from regular accounting?"

"My career is a specialty, where we dig deep into the financials to uncover fraud."

Shanice's face flushed hot at the words *dig deep*. She swallowed. "Fascinating," she croaked.

"You think so? You're the first woman to ever call my work fascinating." His eyes studied her with interest.

"Really? I bet you have all kinds of stories to tell."

"I do, but like I said, most women..." He shrugged.

She couldn't believe this man had difficulty finding interested women. First of all, were they blind? Did they not notice the hollowed cheeks that emphasized his high cheekbones, or the hard jawline and kissable-looking lips? Second of all, she really did believe his work must be interesting.

"You've probably met the wrong kind of women," Shanice said. Then she froze—her heart, her blood, her entire body. She stared at him. Had she said too much?

He didn't respond right away, and a brief moment of awkward silence enveloped them until he spoke again. "Maybe I have," he said quietly.

Her heart restarted.

"It was nice talking to you..." His eyes fell to the name tag over her left breast. "Shanice. Did I say that right?"

"Yes, that's correct."

"Shanice," he murmured again, as if savoring the word. "I

should get going. I have a long night ahead with all this reading."

What? He didn't have plans? Neither did she—if you didn't count reading her latest book, too. They were two sides of the same coin.

"Good night," she said, acutely disappointed their conversation was coming to an end. But she quietly rejoiced because it was the longest one they'd had, and she learned a little about him in those few minutes.

He hesitated, or so it seemed, before he nodded and walked away. And oh, how she enjoyed watching him walk away.

Shanice bit her bottom lip.

No ring on his finger, and probably no girlfriend, either. He liked to read. He was an accountant. Safe. Much different from the life she'd escaped in Texas.

If she were going to start dating again, he was darn near perfect.

4

Shanice drove her blue Ford Taurus slowly down the quiet street to the house where she rented a room. Most of the homes were two-story dwellings with limited yard space and contained families—except for the one directly across the street.

The owner of that one was a twenty-five-year-old who ran a tech company out of his house. He seemed to have a party every night. Cars always lined both sides of the street, and on nights he and his friends hung outside on the back deck, the scent of weed filled the air.

Shanice groaned quietly as she pulled up. Once again, he had lots of company over, forcing her to drive slowly to avoid hitting one of the cars. Two scantily clad women giggled as they ran up to his door arm-in-arm.

She pulled into the driveway and hit the garage door opener. As the door slowly rose, she watched the women in the rear-view mirror. A slender man opened the door from the inside, and she caught a glimpse of the foyer and a man and woman in a liplock near the stairs before the door closed again.

She couldn't help being a little jealous. At least they had something to do on a Friday night. She parked her car next to Beatrice's white Mercedes and entered the kitchen. Beatrice was in there wearing a silk robe, her gray hair tucked under a white silk night cap, one of at least ten she owned. She stood in front of the huge island in the middle of the spacious kitchen eating grapes in a bowl. Her Corgi, Charlie, looked quite relaxed—the opposite of his usual playful self—tucked under her left arm.

"Good night, Beatrice. Hey, Charlie."

"Good night, hon," Beatrice said, smiling fondly at her.

Beatrice was a godsend and treated Shanice like family. When Shanice started working for her at the bookstore and she learned that Shanice was staying at a motel, she offered to rent her a room in her house. The arrangement worked perfectly for Shanice.

Six weeks in, she'd learned a lot about her landlord. The older woman was wealthy, but The Bookish Attic was not where she made her money. The shop was a passion project.

As a young woman, she'd invested heavily in stocks, and over decades those stocks had appreciated. Coupled with a pension, she was a very rich woman living a comfortable life in her seventies.

"How was your day?" Shanice asked.

"Wonderful. Charlie had a good day, too. I took him with me when I went shopping at Merrick Park. I bought a couple of blouses at Ann Taylor. I'll have to show them to you."

"Definitely, I'd love to see them."

"I also met one of my gal pals for an early dinner. How was your day?"

"Great." Shanice picked two grapes from the bowl and popped them in her mouth. "We sold four of those coffee table books that are thirty-five dollars, but other than that, it was a normal day at the store."

"I'm not just talking about the store, dear. I'm talking about you. The past few days you've seemed a bit off."

"Oh." Shanice averted her eyes and entered the walk-in pantry. "I have a lot on my mind, to be honest. But I'm fine."

"Are you sure?"

"Yes."

Shanice exited the pantry with a bag of sweet potato chips.

"Good, then I won't feel guilty about leaving you again."

"Where are you going now?" Shanice asked.

One of the benefits of living with Beatrice was that she and Charlie traveled often, which meant every week or two, Shanice had the house to herself for a few days.

"It's a last-minute thing. You know Velma, my friend over at Shady Pines? Well, she and another friend were supposed to go on a cruise, but the friend backed out at the last minute. Can you believe that? I'm not surprised, though, since Velma admitted that her so-called friend had not yet paid for her part of the trip. I keep telling her she's too kind to people and they'll keep taking advantage of her. Anyway, she asked if I could take her friend's place. Of course, I had nothing coming up or important to do, so I agreed. We leave day after tomorrow, on a cruise to South America. Charlie and I will be gone for two weeks."

"Wow, that's a long time."

"It's the longest I've been away since you moved in. Will you be all right?" She looked genuinely concerned, which warmed Shanice's heart.

She touched Beatrice's shoulder. "I'll be fine. I'm just a little jealous. I want to be you when I grow up, able to drop every-thing and take a trip whenever I feel like it." She sighed dramatically.

Beatrice laughed. "Follow my investment advice, and you'll be able to, my dear." She scooped up the bowl of grapes. "Have a good night." Beatrice headed out of the kitchen.

"Good night," Shanice called after her.

In the silence of the kitchen, she smiled. She was happy for Beatrice. She'd never married or had kids but was living her best life. Maybe that was something Shanice had to look forward to, though she wanted to start living her best life *now*.

She poured a glass of water, dropped in two ice cubes, and after tucking the bag of chips under her arm, turned out the light. Upstairs in her bedroom, her mind drifted to Vicente. He'd occupied way too much of her thoughts, but his visits to the store made him hard to forget.

She still remembered the first time he'd come in. He'd caught her eye then, even before he said a word. And when he spoke, her knees had practically knocked together.

There was something about him. He was different from any other man she'd met, and after talking to him in more detail tonight, she'd become even more curious. She would love to know more about his background, his likes and dislikes. They enjoyed the same reading material, and she wondered what else they had in common.

Shanice kicked off her shoes and dialed her mother's number. When Miriam answered the phone, there was a lot of lively chatter in the background.

"Hey, honey. I didn't think I would hear from you tonight." She heard a smile in her mother's voice.

"Apparently. Sounds like you're having a party." Shanice sat on the bed and pulled some chips from the bag.

Her mother laughed. "I have a few friends over. It's supposed to be our book club meeting, but it turned into a party."

"I guess that's because you guys always have so much wine and food at these so-called book club meetings. I'm pretty sure they're just a reason for you to party every month." She crunched a sweet potato chip between her teeth.

There was a peal of laughter in the background, and her

mother said to someone, "Wait! Don't tell them yet. I want to hear the whole story from the beginning."

Voices yelled back at her, but Shanice couldn't understand what they said.

"Mom, you sound like you're busy. I'll call you another day."

"I'm never too busy for you. Hold on." After a few seconds, the noise in the background became distant, and then she heard a door close, and the chatter and laughter disappeared altogether.

"Are you okay?" Miriam asked.

"I'm fine. I shouldn't have bothered you."

"Honey, I told you you're not bothering me. What's going on? I know something is wrong because I can hear it in your voice."

Now she felt silly. She wanted someone to talk to but was too embarrassed to tell her mother how lonely she felt. She couldn't even go to see her because she didn't want to risk getting her involved in what she had gotten herself tangled up in. Besides, her mother deserved to have fun, and the monthly meetings helped her get out of her funk since Shanice's father died. Didn't she deserve to be happy? Of course she did.

"Tell you what, go back to spending time with your friends. I'll call you tomorrow when you're free to talk."

"I'm free now," her mother insisted.

"No, you're not, and really, neither am I. I just got in from work, and I'm tired, so I'm going to take a shower and go straight to bed, okay?"

"If you're sure," Miriam said slowly, her voice laced with doubt.

"I'm sure, Mom. Have fun, and tell auntie Joan I said hi."

"She keeps asking me when you're going to come see her," her mother said.

"I can't right now, but as soon as I can get away from the store, I promise, I'll come for a visit."

"Okay, sweetie. Love you."

"Love you, too."

Shanice went into the bathroom and took a quick shower. She hadn't completely lied to her mother about being tired. Fatigue squeezed her shoulders, but it wasn't only physical. It was a mental fatigue that came off and on, ever since she left Texas and moved here. For a little while she wanted to escape from the heaviness of the thoughts that plagued her.

She thought about Vicente again—his hands, and what they would feel like on her skin. What would it be like if she could let go and allow him to do whatever he wanted to her?

Shanice rubbed soap over her tightening nipples.

"What is wrong with you?" she whispered to herself, shaking her head. Was she so hard up for sex that she couldn't stop thinking about that customer? Yes, apparently so. A man who very possibly had a girlfriend, they just didn't have plans tonight.

After her shower, she dressed in purple pajama shorts and a matching top. Then she lay in the bed, staring up at the ceiling. She didn't have much. Beatrice had supplied the bed and five-drawer bureau where she kept the few clothes she brought with her. She'd fled Texas with very little, taking the bus and buying an older model Ford Taurus with cash when she arrived in town.

Maybe she was more tired than she realized, or maybe it was the stress of her predicament, but she soon felt drowsy.

Her eyelids lowered, her mind wandering to the situation she'd gotten herself into. She still didn't know what to do but was pretty sure she'd made the right decision to leave Houston. She felt safer here, far away from the danger. She stayed under the radar, using only cash and no credit cards. She'd even gotten rid of her phone, and the new one was in her mother's name. She'd done all that to avoid leaving any type of trail that would make it easy for her to be tracked down.

"Trust no one," Dennis had told her, and the fear in his eyes and voice had frightened her. "I'm pretty sure they've killed before."

"What have you gotten yourself into?" she'd asked.

"Don't worry about that. But if I can finish what I started, I'll be famous."

"*If.*"

"Yeah. If," he'd agreed.

Like she'd promised, Shanice hadn't said a word, but she was very much afraid, and not being able to tell anyone her secret made her feel alone.

At some point, she'd have to tell *someone* what she knew. But who could she trust? Dennis had made it sound as if no one in law enforcement could be trusted. At least she'd bought herself time by moving here.

But at some point, she had to figure out what to do next.

5

"Good night!" Shanice waved at Ava as she climbed into her car.

Shortly afterward, she parked outside the supermarket and grabbed a tote bag from the back seat. This was her Saturday night ritual—leave work, pick up groceries for the next few days. She could order out, but that was a splurge reserved for rare occasions. She was way too careful with the money she spent, and eating out added up.

Besides, she wanted to move from Miami and hadn't been completely honest with Vicente. True, she liked the beaches and the people and the weather, but she couldn't see herself staying there indefinitely. She'd come here on a whim because she'd visited before. The familiar city seemed like the right place to temporarily escape to, but she longed to settle down somewhere quiet. She still wasn't sure where she'd go exactly. Maybe Bradenton or one of the smaller towns in Florida, or even out of state.

Shanice browsed the produce, lifting and examining tomatoes, lettuce, and other veggies for the big salad she had planned. She'd make enough for dinner and lunch tomorrow, and any leftover vegetables could be used in a stir-fry with some chicken for tomorrow night's dinner.

Sauntering over to the fruit, she eyed organic strawberries and smiled at a toddler who waved from a cart. She dismissed the strawberries. They spoiled too fast, and she wouldn't eat them all in time.

She mentally went through the list of items she came to pick up, laughing at herself as she realized she almost forgot the most important ingredient—the meat.

She went over to the chicken and picked up some skinless chicken breasts. *Or maybe a ribeye tonight,* she thought, eyeing the options. She picked up one with nice marbling running through the lean.

"Shanice?"

She turned and quietly gasped when she saw Vicente. He still wore his glasses, but he wore basketball shorts that put his thick calves on display, and a gunmetal-gray long-sleeved cotton shirt shoved up to the elbows exposed meaty-looking forearms sprinkled with dark hair. He looked bigger and stronger. He looked like he wrestled bears for a living.

Dang. What did he do in his spare time when he wasn't crunching numbers? He must work out *a lot.*

"*Hiiii.*" Ugh. What was she, a preteen meeting her celebrity crush? She hoped she didn't sound too eager and cleared her throat. "Hi," she repeated in a firmer voice. "What are you doing here?" She'd seen him earlier when he came into the store, but she'd been busy with a customer and they didn't get a chance to chat like last night.

He flashed a gorgeous smile. "I was about to ask you the same thing. I stop here every so often because it's near my apartment. Do you live nearby?"

"About ten minutes away. Like you, it's conveniently near

where I live, so sometimes I stop by and grab groceries that I need. Tonight I'm having a steak salad." She held up the package of ribeye and then dropped it into her basket.

"Sounds good. So, you like to cook...?" Eyes scanning the contents of the basket in her hand, he seemed very interested in her culinary skills.

"A little. It's certainly cheaper than eating out all the time, and convenient. How about you?" She peeked into his hand basket and saw canned goods, jars of spaghetti sauce, and boxes of pasta.

"I love to cook, actually. Plus cooking can be really relaxing."

She nodded. "I agree. What's for dinner tonight?" She wanted to keep him around, to continue listening to his sexy, accented voice and stare at his incredible body.

"Tonight I'm keeping it simple. I've had ground beef defrosting in the refrigerator since yesterday. I picked up spaghetti sauce and pasta, so I'm having Italian. Although, cooking for one means I'll be eating spaghetti and meat sauce for the next few days. It's cheap but plentiful." He was more relaxed and talkative and smiled a lot.

Shanice laughed. "Well, at least you planned ahead, which makes you much smarter than me, which is why I'm standing here at the steaks." Her mouth twisted into a rueful expression of regret, prompting a laugh from him.

It was brief, yet the sound touched a place deep in her chest, squeezing as if with an iron fist. What she'd been aching for, what was missing from her life could be standing right before her and she couldn't make a move because she didn't know what the future held. She might have to move again tomorrow.

She used to be confident and self-assured, but now she couldn't trust her own judgment—couldn't definitely say the sun was shining even when its bright rays lit up the sky. She was *that* unsure of herself ever since the fiasco with Dennis.

"Is something wrong?" Vicente asked.

Shanice had forgotten he was standing in front of her. His question and expression of frowning concern snapped her out of her morbid thoughts. "No, I'm fine. Got lost in thought for a minute. So, you don't make your own spaghetti sauce?"

He chuckled. "I can cook, but I like the easy route. Of course, I buy the jarred version and end up cutting up basil, onions, and garlic to flavor it, so I should probably make it from scratch anyway." He shrugged.

"I'm the same. Don't be too hard on yourself."

A pause filled the space between them.

Vicente shifted from one foot to the next. "I...I'll let you go back to your shopping. I need to pick up a few more things before I go home, but I had to come over and say hello."

"I'm glad you did, and it was nice to see you."

"Yes. Twice in one day, and you live nearby."

"I do." She nodded.

He watched her for a moment, and she remained still under his scrutiny. She barely noticed the other shoppers passing by, she was so taken with him and their conversation. Vicente seemed deep in thought, but then must have made a decision, because he heaved a breath. "I'll see you around. Well, definitely at the bookstore."

"Yes, definitely." Shanice pushed down the hot surge of disappointment.

"Good night."

"Good night."

She watched him walk away with a throb of pain in her heart. The ache to say something, to call out to him, never manifested into any action. With regret, she turned back to the meat, scouring the options for chicken this time.

"Shanice?" Surprised, she swung around at the sound of her name again. This time, Vicente seemed more hesitant. She could see it in his eyes. What did this hunk of man have to be hesitant about?

"Yes?" she asked, anticipation making her voice breathless.

He laughed softly, nervously, his gaze sweeping up and down the aisle, as if searching for the confidence he needed to say what was on the tip of his tongue.

She held her breath. Waiting.

His gaze met hers again. "Are you seeing anyone? Do you have a boyfriend?"

"No." Her fingers tightened on the basket handle. *Ohmigod, ohmigod, ohmigod.*

"Would you, er...would you be interested in going out with me? Maybe dinner?"

"Sure. I'm free next Saturday."

"I was thinking sooner. Tomorrow night?"

She didn't have to work Sunday night, but hesitated. What did she really know about this man? Nothing, really, and she was about to spend time with him. But how else would she get to know him if she didn't spend time with him?

"You know what, I'm being too pushy. I'm sorry, I—"

"No, I'd love to go out with you," Shanice hastily said.

"Are you sure?"

"Yes, I'm sure. And I don't have a boyfriend, since I plan to spend the night cuddling with my salad and a good book."

A smile stretched across his face. "I have similar plans. Well then, dinner...tomorrow night, right?"

"Yes," Shanice said with a laugh. She couldn't believe how hesitant he was. Some woman or women had really done a number on his self-confidence.

"We should exchange numbers."

"Oh, yes!"

They handed each other their phones and plugged in their names and numbers, then handed them back.

Vicente grinned. "Well, I'm glad I stopped by the store tonight. I almost decided to pick up a meal at a restaurant, but now I'm glad I didn't. I would have missed running into you."

"I'm glad you didn't do that, too."

"I need time to think of a good place to eat, so I'll give you a call tomorrow afternoon, if that works?"

"That works."

"Perfect. I'm looking forward to our date."

"Me, too," Shanice admitted softly.

This time when he walked away, she didn't take her eyes off him until he'd disappeared down an aisle.

Bouncing on her feet, Shanice practically skipped to the checkout. She wouldn't get too involved with him. That would be foolish, especially if she had to leave town. But she could have fun, right? Of course she could.

She couldn't stop smiling.

Seated in a gray Nissan outside in the parking lot, Cruz watched as Shanice exited the store with swaying hips and a bounce in her step. She climbed into her blue Taurus and took off, and he took off behind her.

She clearly had no idea that he'd been following her for the past week, and even if she thought she was being followed, she would dismiss it.

The average person had very little situational awareness, and people often dismissed any uneasy feelings that suggested something was wrong in their immediate vicinity—completely overriding their instincts, nature's way of keeping them alive. That made surveillance easy when dealing with civilians.

He knew every route that took him to and away from the

house where she lived on a dead-end street. He'd followed her to and from work, as well as out to dinner one night with her co-worker, Ava.

Knowing that she was so unaware of her surroundings concerned him. Other forces wanted that data, and if they hadn't found her yet, he worried that they'd find her eventually.

Cruz frowned. What was he doing being worried about her? For all he knew, she was an accomplice with Dennis or in cahoots with the people who'd killed him. He needed to think with his head and not his dick—which wasn't easy with a woman who looked like her.

He pulled onto her street, the number of cars parked around her house posing a minor irritation, but since the house across the street was always busy, it made blending in easier.

He drove past her house as Shanice pulled into the garage, completely unaware of his presence. Furthermore, she didn't seem to suspect that he was anything more than an accountant, which meant his cover was working.

Because of his size and build, he'd found ways to come across less intimidating. Glasses, a loose-fitting shirt, and a shuffle to his walk instead of a confident stride were all important pieces of the Vicente cover. He'd even pitched his voice a little higher and used well-placed hesitation when he spoke instead of his usual low-timbered, confident voice.

What wasn't fake was his interest in Shanice. She exuded warmth and sex appeal without trying. Her full breasts were more than a handful, and her ass was spectacular, especially in the form-fitting dress she wore tonight. He'd watched her from behind for a long time before he finally called her name.

She also had a sweet voice, and every time she spoke he felt compelled to pay attention. And her laughter...well, that was a bonus, as welcome as the sun's rays pushing between storm clouds.

Mierda, he needed to stop browsing the poetry section. If he wasn't careful, he'd be writing his own lines soon.

Cruz did a U-turn at the end of the street and then drove back toward her house. Nothing seemed out of place.

He left the subdivision and headed back to his apartment.

6

Shanice exited the cab and climbed the steps to La Cocina Patagonia in the Patagonia Hotel. The popular restaurant was located on a quiet end of South Beach and served South American food. Thanks to an Argentine owner, they had a reputation for great steaks, and the owner's wife, a sommelier, had curated a wine list that offered excellent choices from vineyards all over the world.

The quiet hum of conversation and the sound of silverware touching plates greeted Shanice as she approached the entrance to the restaurant. She saw Vicente right away, towering over the maître d', an older Hispanic man wearing a dark suit and gold tie.

Vicente looked absolutely delicious in a black jacket and black and white striped tie, and when he turned toward her, her breath hitched, and she broke into a smile. He smiled back, softening his features and making her heart jumpstart like a horse breaking free at the starting gate.

"You look nice," she said.

His gaze roved over her in a slow, measured way that heated

her skin. "And you look...incredible." One corner of his mouth tipped upward into a crooked smile.

His compliment pleased her since she'd spent a lot of time on her appearance. She wore a leopard print top and black slacks, and she'd washed and deep-conditioned her curly hair, making sure every single strand looked perfect. Not a single bit of frizz in sight.

Without warning, Vicente slipped a hand around her waist and leaned close to her ear. "In Spanish, I would say, *t'eres un mango*. That means you're hot."

Shanice blushed. He smelled so good—like leather and citrus. She really, really wanted to get this guy naked and get that scent all over her skin. She hadn't had sex in months, making it hard to be good right now.

Shanice tipped back her head to look up at him. "You'll have to teach me more Spanish words."

"I intend to. I'm glad you came, Shanice. I wasn't sure you would. When you said you wanted to meet me here instead of letting me pick you up, I assumed that was your sneaky way of getting out of the date."

"Once you get to know me, you'll learn that I only say what I mean. If I didn't want to come on this date, I would have told you."

His eyes sparkled with interest. "Good to know."

They followed a hostess through the middle of the restaurant to a table that looked out onto the back street where cars cruised by and the neon lights of a local hotel painted each vehicle with red and green as they passed. After they were settled, a waiter came over. Dark-skinned, with a Spanish accent similar to Vicente's, he introduced himself as Marco and took their drink orders. After he left them alone, Shanice stole a peek at her date, whose head was bent over the menu. His wavy black hair looked luxurious under the recessed lights.

She couldn't remember the last time she'd sat down with a

man on an actual date over dinner and wine. The last time she'd been out with a man was with Dennis, and he'd taken her to an off-the-beaten-path restaurant because he was worried about his wife seeing them together while they were in the middle of a divorce. Being out in the open and dressed up was a nice change.

"Any suggestions?" she asked, dropping her gaze to the menu.

The dishes ranged from Peruvian ceviche to grilled Argentine meats, and included interesting choices for dessert. Everything sounded delicious, and she had a hard time deciding what to order.

"I have no idea," Vicente admitted.

"Is this your first time here?"

He finally looked up. "Yes. We'll be discovering this place together."

"You made a risky decision bringing me here," she said.

"How so?"

"Aren't you trying to impress me?" She batted her eyelashes at him.

He chuckled. "I thought *you* were trying to impress me," he teased.

"I am. I guess the desire to impress goes both ways."

"I think you're right." His gaze flicked to the menu again and then he set it aside. "I have an idea. Why don't we forget about the menu and have the waiter decide what we'll eat and drink tonight."

"Oooh, that's really living on the edge. I don't know."

"Are you in?"

Without hesitation, Shanice folded her menu. "I'm in."

Cruz took it, and when Marco returned, he handed both to him. "We're being daredevils tonight. We want you to order for us. What do your customers usually enjoy? Whatever that is, we want it."

The waiter grinned. "You're sure about this?"

"I'm sure. We want the works—appetizers, entree, a nice bottle of wine, and if we have room at the end of the meal, dessert." He looked directly at her. "This is our first date, and I'm trying to impress her."

"Your first date?" The man's grin widened as he looked at Shanice, and then he said something to Cruz in Spanish. Cruz replied, they both laughed, and the waiter left the table.

"What was *that* about?" Shanice asked, spreading her napkin across her lap.

"I shouldn't tell you."

"You have to tell me. It would be really rude if you didn't."

"You're right. He said that you're a very beautiful woman and I'm a very lucky man."

"Did he really say that?" Shanice asked, her cheeks heating with color.

"Yes, he did."

"And what did you say?"

"I said, 'I know. So make sure you make me look good tonight.'" His eyes sparkled with humor.

"I'm...flattered," Shanice said. She ran a fingertip up and down the stem of her water glass.

Vicente stopped her movements by taking her hand.

"Tell me about you, Shanice. I want to know everything."

"How far back do you want me to go?"

"Don't go as far back as the womb and we should be fine."

She laughed. "You surprise me. You have a sense of humor, which wasn't obvious initially."

"I try." He smiled.

Man, those lips.

"There's not much to tell. I don't have a lot of family, except my mother, as I mentioned. My father, who passed away a few years ago, was a cognitive psychologist, or what some people simply call a brain scientist. He was a brilliant man, always reading and studying, constantly curious about how the brain works and how we remember things and learn. His second love was chemistry, and that occupied much of his time, too. He loved tinkering in his lab at home."

"He had a lab at home? That sounds dangerous."

She enjoyed his touch as he idly played with her fingers. His thick fingers were rougher than she expected for an accountant, as if he worked a lot with his hands. She didn't mind the roughness, though. It added another intriguing dimension to the man and made her want to learn more about him.

"Oh, it was, and it drove my mother crazy. Initially the lab was a room at the back of the house, but after a small fire that resulted in charred walls and a panicked call to the fire department before we were able to put it out, she banished him to outside. He ended up building a shed in the back yard, and I used to spend a lot of time out there with him as his assistant. I learned so much, not only about science but about life. We talked about everything." Her heart ached, and she wondered if she'd ever fully recover from no longer having him in her life.

Vicente gently squeezed her hand and brought her attention back to him. "I'm sorry for your loss."

"Thank you." She heaved a sigh. "Anyway, my parents had that kind of crazy love, where no one else matters in the world but that person. They met in college, fell in love, got married, and lived happily until cancer stole my dad from us. But while we had him, he blessed our lives in all kinds of ways, and I really miss him."

The waiter arrived with a bottle of red wine. After they tasted it, he poured them each a glass and promised to return with their appetizers before too long.

Vicente took another sip of wine before setting his glass on the table. "When you talk about your parents' relationship, you sound wistful."

"Do I?" Shanice laughed. "Being with someone you really connect with can be absolutely amazing, when it's right. I saw that with them."

Folding his arms on the table, he asked, "Why are you still single?"

Shanice wrinkled her nose. "Yuck. Why do men ask that awful question?"

"I'm sorry. Do we?"

"So many times."

"Maybe because we can't believe it when we find an incredible woman like you who's single, and we genuinely want to know. I know I do."

She felt a little guilty. The truth was, she didn't want to talk about why she wasn't in a relationship, but sitting in the quiet ambiance of La Cocina Patagonia, with a glass of red wine and a handsome man who looked as if he genuinely cared about her answer, her resolve softened.

"I haven't been in a relationship in a while. My last one ended abruptly, and I've been single ever since."

"I see," he said slowly. "Are you still heartbroken over him?"

She shook her head vehemently. "Hate I'd wasted my time, to be honest."

Brown eyes met umber eyes across the table.

"Relationships aren't easy."

"No, they're not," Shanice agreed.

Marco reappeared with a waitress trailing behind him and holding a tray on her shoulder.

"Your appetizers are here," he said.

The young woman lowered the tray and Marco removed a white dish and set it carefully in the center of the table. "These are two of our meat empanadas, which are legendary on the strip. You will not find a better empanada anywhere. And this is our ceviche." He placed oversized martini glasses filled with fish and shrimp in front of each of them. "I'm sure you'll be very satisfied with your choices. Can I get you anything else?"

"Nothing for me." Shanice looked across the table at Vicente.

He shook his head, and Marco and the waitress left.

"I'm going to be full off the appetizers alone," Shanice remarked. She bit into one of the empanadas and crossed her eyes at the delicious flavor. "Mmm, he's right, this is so good."

"So he didn't steer us wrong so far, eh?" Vicente bit into his.

"No, he did good."

"I guess I'm on my way to impressing you," he said.

Shanice's lips broke into a smile. "I guess you are."

7

Cruz checked his watch as he waited for Shanice to return from the restroom.

Dinner had been exceptional. He had wolfed down his steak and lobster, and Shanice had danced in her seat as she devoured a meal of grilled steak topped with jumbo shrimp served with a side of vegetables.

Over the course of the meal, they'd discussed books and poetry, but every time she tried to learn more about him, he deftly turned the conversation back to her. He wondered if she'd had any idea Dennis was married. She'd seemed genuinely upset about the end of their relationship, but that didn't mean she was being completely honest. He'd been working covert operations long enough to know that people were good actors.

Shanice came toward the table, her buxom build causing a few male eyes to follow her across the floor. Out of nowhere, a surge of jealousy made Cruz clench his fist. He had no claims to this woman. This was simply a job like any other, but the thought of other men imagining her naked the same way he was irritated the hell out of him.

When an older man caught Cruz staring him down, he immediately lowered his gaze to his plate.

Standing, he said, "I already paid the bill. Ready to go?"

"Ready," Shanice said.

As they walked out, he placed a hand at her lower back, telling himself the possessive move was him simply playing the part he'd been assigned, but knowing full well there was a deeper meaning behind the act.

"Would you like to go for a walk?" he asked.

She glanced up at him, eyes bright with pleasure. "I'd love to."

They said good night to the maître d' and exited the hotel. They crossed the street to the side that bordered the water and strolled toward the more boisterous end of South Beach, where people showed off their sports cars and loud salsa music poured from the front entrance of some of the restaurants.

"What kind of work did you do before you started at the bookstore?" he asked.

"I'm not answering any more questions. I've talked about myself all night."

"I don't mind." He really didn't, as everything she said helped him put together pieces of the puzzle that was Shanice.

"I want to know about *you*."

"We're not talking about me. We're talking about you right now."

"Nope. I'm not used to one-sided conversation, and I have questions, too."

Give and take would be important to building trust between them. "What do you want to know?"

"For starters, why are *you* still single?"

In his line of work, lies and half-truths were the norm, but the key was to tell as much of the truth as possible so you didn't have to remember a lie.

"Work," Cruz answered.

He sat down on a bench directly across the street from a restaurant with its doors open and a blue light waving across the façade. Guests dined at the tables on the sidewalk while others loitered with drinks in hand around the outdoor bar that faced a bubbling fountain. The scene looked less like a restaurant and more like a discotheque.

Shanice joined him. "Do you like your job?"

Stretching his right arm along the back of the bench behind her back, he said, "I do. I've done it for years. It's brutal, but interesting, and also very time-consuming. It doesn't leave much time for a family."

"Wow, I had no idea accounting was such demanding work. I know it can be grueling during tax season."

Cruz nodded. "I stay busy all year."

His work was intense and dirty, but enjoyable. Though he couldn't imagine doing anything else, there were times when he wondered about his life choices. What else could he do with his skillsets and not have to start over?

Remaining in this line of work meant not allowing anyone to get too close. He couldn't have a family. Who would want a man like him—a killer? To kill you had to practically be devoid of feelings and completely dedicated to the completion of the mission. Wives, girlfriends, and kids created a burden.

"The bookstore ebbs and flows. I love my job, too. Being around words all day is wonderful, and I get to share that love with people like you."

She blushed and looked down at her lap.

All of a sudden the night took on a different air, and he wondered what it would be like to be on a real date with Shanice. What if this weren't a job?

His chest tightened. That was unusual—for him to feel emotion toward anyone, particularly someone he was working for information. He needed to stay focused.

"Why did you ask me out?"

That shift in the air deepened, and he saw the longing in her eyes. He almost didn't speak, but then he heard himself say, "Why not? You have an amazing smile, and you were always friendly every time I came into your store. You have a great personality, and tonight I've learned you're easy to talk to."

Nothing he'd said had been a lie. He meant every word. Shanice had a glow about her and an appealing personality that he could see easily drawing people in. She hadn't been kind to only him at the bookstore. He'd seen her treat other customers the same way.

"And you're very, very sexy," he added gutturally.

"Sexy?" she repeated with raised eyebrows.

"Yes." He meant that, too.

"You're very sexy, too," she said in a soft voice.

As clear as day, he saw she wanted him to kiss her. Her full lips were slightly parted and her eyes became hooded as she gazed up at him. His loins tightened with suppressed need. He wanted this woman, badly. But his job to get close to her did not include tonguing her down on a bench in the middle of South Beach.

And he knew it wouldn't be enough. His tongue would want a taste of her breasts. He had a sudden urge to lick her nipples, to take them one at a time into his mouth and suck to his heart's content.

Fighting the urge with Herculean strength, he stood abruptly. "It's getting late. I should take you home."

CRUZ PARKED in front of the garage and then walked behind Shanice to the front door. As he did, his eyes swept the area. Nothing seemed out of the ordinary, but he paid attention to each of the houses and quickly analyzed but dismissed the many cars parked on either side of the street. Four of them he recognized from previous nights.

"Is your neighbor having a party?" he asked, as if he hadn't been in her neighborhood before.

"Every night. He's very popular."

At the door, Shanice turned to face him and clasped her hands in front of her. "I had a wonderful evening."

"I did, too," he admitted, swallowing the ball of tension in his throat.

He knew better than to get attached, yet he had a moment of regret—regret that very soon this charade would be over and he'd have to leave her behind, assuming she wasn't somehow involved in this sordid mess.

Shanice grasped his striped tie and pulled his head down to hers. He gripped either side of the door and his whole body tensed. He hadn't slept with a woman in a long time. Infrequent and sporadic hookups were the norm, and he wanted inside her so badly, he was liable to hurt her the first time if he ever got the chance.

"How about a kiss goodnight? I don't mind. I promise," she whispered. Rising on tiptoe, she pressed her lips against his.

Immediately, his body reacted, like some carnal beast. His fingers tightened on the doorframe so as not to crush her against him, because he had to exhibit some level of control.

Her tongue flicked against the seam of his mouth, and he reluctantly opened. The moment she entered, he sucked hard and angled his head to the side. She pressed against him, sliding her arms around his neck. His dick throbbed and his entire body ached with the need to give in and dive into her delectably plump body.

Unable to resist any longer, one arm banded around her waist and locked her in place against him. He devoured her lips, his tongue forging into the sweet cavern of her mouth, as one hand explored her soft curves.

Taking encouragement from the mewling noises she made, he molded the lines of her body with his hands—traveling over her back and hips before coming to rest on her wonderfully fat ass.

He knew better than to get involved with an asset, but there he was, shoving his tongue down her throat and grabbing her like he was tossed at sea and her ass was his lifesaver. With one final squeeze of her butt cheeks, he did the sensible thing and pulled back.

"I think you better go inside," he rasped.

She fisted her fingers around his tie, and her lips curved into an enticing smile right before she pressed their coolness against his throat. "You have way too much self-control, Vicente," she whispered.

Suddenly, he hated that name with a passion. He hated the glasses. He hated the wall between them, created by his hidden identity. He wanted her to know him and say his real name, breathing it in that same husky voice she'd just done his fake one.

Her tongue traced up the length of his Adam's apple, and shivers ran up his spine. He was strong, but he wasn't a damn robot.

Cruz grabbed the back of her neck with his right hand while the left grabbed a handful of her ass and hauled her tight against his rock-hard erection.

She gasped, eyes going wide.

"On the contrary, it seems I have very little control where you're concerned."

His mouth slammed down on hers. Her throat squeaked out a whimper as all her softness was crushed against his hard body. But she gave as good as she got, the sounds of their hungry kisses filling the quiet of the night at her front door. He pressed her against the hard surface and would have done much more if the sound of a car backfiring as it drove by didn't penetrate the fog of lust.

With deep regret, he tore his mouth away from hers, nostrils flaring, his jaw tightening with the immense effort not to lift her against the door and fuck her till she wept from pleasure.

Shanice whimpered, clinging to him by tightening her arms around his neck.

"I'd better go," he whispered.

Her chest heaved and her eyes were clouded over with the same desire that raged through his blood. She rested her head against his chest where she could certainly hear his pounding heart.

"Too bad," she whispered.

Yes, too bad.

"Keys," Cruz commanded.

She moaned and handed them over.

"Which one?"

"That." She pointed at the one with a green key cap on top of it.

Rubbing her back, he said, "I want to stay, but it's best that I go. I have an early work day tomorrow. Don't you have to work?"

She nodded. "Unfortunately."

He opened the door and then handed over her keys.

She looked up at him with forlorn eyes.

He chuckled softly. Her unhappiness stroked his ego, but he couldn't stay. "I had a great time tonight. I'll call you tomorrow. I promise."

"All right." Shanice stepped into the doorway and rested her cheek against the frame as she gazed out at him.

"I'll call you tomorrow," he promised again.

"You better. Good night."

"Good night."

Cruz waited until she shut the door and then went to his car. Inside, he fished a little metal container out of his pocket and opened it. The box contained Blu Tack, a putty-like adhesive he'd pressed her door key into. He'd made a flawless copy, which meant easy access when he came by tomorrow to enter her house.

Cruz snapped the lid closed and stuffed the container back into his pocket. He backed out to the edge of the driveway and paused, eyes lingering on the lighted window at the front. She was upstairs getting ready for bed.

He could be up there with her if...

Cruz stopped himself from going down that road and instead did a quick visual scan of the street. Once again, nothing seemed amiss.

He removed the glasses once he'd driven away from the house and then turned onto the next street. Leaving her had been hard—the hardest thing he'd had to do in a long time.

8

C ruz sat in a rented car at a gas station one hundred feet from the entrance to Shanice's subdivision. At fifteen minutes to eight, her blue Taurus came out and headed in the direction of the bookstore. She didn't notice him, didn't so much as look in his direction.

Since she told him her roommate, Beatrice, and the dog were on a cruise, the house should be empty. Tapping his fingers on the steering wheel, he waited another ten minutes to be sure she didn't double back, and then drove into the subdivision.

He kept his eyes on the other houses as he cruised down the street. The only house probably occupied right now was the one owned by the tech guy. Cruz had gotten information on him already and knew he was harmless. The people in the houses immediately surrounding Shanice's residence also checked out.

He'd watched the families on either side of her house leave earlier. On the left, the husband and wife drove away in the same car. The house on the right, the mother took her daughter in the car with her, about twenty minutes before her husband pulled out of the subdivision, probably on his way to work.

Cruz pulled into the driveway like he belonged there and climbed out carrying a small leather bag in hand, which contained a variety of tools.

Homeowners who paid for alarm systems thought their homes were secure—and they were, to some degree. But the sad truth was, wireless alarms were woefully easy to circumvent. The systems all suffered from the same weakness: they relied on radio frequency signals, but the signals weren't encrypted, which made it easy for someone like him to intercept and decipher the data and use it however he wished.

He'd been watching the house ever since he arrived in Miami, so he'd taken care of capturing the data days before. As he took the walkway to the front door, key in hand, his brain replayed the stolen code he would need to disarm the alarm.

Cruz turned the key in the lock and walked into the house as if he owned it. The alarm beeped at him as he shut the door, and he punched in the code to turn it off. He waited in the silence, listening for movement or any other sounds that indicated the house wasn't truly empty. One could never be too careful. He heard nothing unusual and confidently moved deeper into the house as he dialed the number to The Bookish Attic, using his Bluetooth so he could keep his hands free.

"The Bookish Attic. This is Shanice, how may I help you?"

He'd thought about her long after they parted ways last night and felt compelled to hear her voice. She sounded so chipper, he smiled.

"Good morning. This is Vicente. I'm at work and thought I'd call and say hello, like I promised."

Important documents or items that needed to be hidden were usually kept in bedrooms—most often, the master. But he started with the rooms downstairs to be sure.

"Hiii," she breathed. "I'm glad you called. I've been thinking about you a lot since last night."

"I've been thinking about you, too." The words burned his tongue, though he wasn't lying. He *had* been thinking about her, but he was deceiving her, nonetheless.

Seeing nothing in the pantry, Cruz went over to the large island in the middle of the kitchen.

"I had such a great time last night. Dinner was great, and I... I like you a lot, Vicente. You came along at the right time, to help me make a decision I'd been hesitant about."

He stopped rummaging through the drawer in the island. "What decision is that?"

"I can't say right now, but are you free tomorrow night?"

"I'm free tonight. I could stop by your house after work."

"I can't tonight. Ava and I have plans. How about tomorrow night?"

"That's fine."

"Good." Her voice lowered. "I have a customer, so I have to go. Have a great day at work!"

"You, too."

Cruz hung up. What was that about?

He completed his search downstairs. Finding nothing, he made his way upstairs. Based on her habit of turning on the light every time she came home from work, he already knew that Shanice's bedroom faced the street. He checked the other bedrooms first, going through Beatrice's nightstand and lifting the clothes in her dresser for a hiding place. The only notable item he found was an envelope of cash pushed between the mattress and the box spring.

The guest bedroom was mostly empty, containing only a full-size bed and an empty five-drawer bureau. He went down the hall to Shanice's bedroom and cracked open the door.

Subtle and wispy, ginger and honey and her own natural body fragrance drifted into his nose. Tension coursed through his muscles, but he shrugged off his tightening body and began his search in the sparsely furnished room.

She didn't have much in the way of personal possessions. No photos on the wall, and the nightstand was empty except for embossed note cards and a few pens. The bed was made with a bright yellow comforter and white sheets, and a laptop rested on the bureau across from it.

The top drawer contained a collection of bras and colorful panties in all styles—lace, cotton, cheekies. He picked up a pair of black panties edged with lace and imagined peeling the soft fabric from her hips.

Fighting a groan, he tossed the underwear back in the drawer and checked the next three. There were pajamas and a couple of nighties, shirts, and other clothing items. The last drawer didn't contain any clothes at all.

He came up empty-handed in the bathroom and bedroom, so next he entered the walk-in closet. It was half full. A shelf at the top of the closet held empty decorative boxes and luggage. He moved them around, and behind a large suitcase, discovered a red backpack.

"What do we have here?" he muttered, lifting it down.

He opened the backpack and examined the contents. This looked suspiciously like a bolt bag, otherwise known as a go bag, the kind of thing he would pack in case he needed to evacuate a city quickly. She had a change of clothes, a flashlight, batteries, matches, and two bottles of water.

Shifting the contents, he saw a black plastic bag at the bottom. He took everything out and removed the bag. His lips tightened when he saw what was inside. Cash. Lots of it, mostly in large bills. Cold dread enveloped his skin as he fanned the money with his thumb. There must be close to fifty thousand dollars there.

He replaced all the items, returned the bag to its previous location behind the suitcase on the top shelf, and stalked out of the closet. Why the hell did Shanice have that much cash on hand?

According to Miles, she'd never once visited Dennis in jail. Could she have turned on him and received cash for the notebook, then bolted? But who would pay for it? Or was she a co-conspirator on the run, afraid that she, too, would end up dead?

He needed answers to those questions, and he needed to find out where the notebook was because it sure as hell wasn't here. Maybe he should tie her up and use threats and intimidation to drag the information from her.

As soon as the thought came, he shunned the idea of violence. He'd find out what he needed to know in a different way. Using the small screwdriver he'd brought in the leather bag, he unscrewed the outlet beside her bed and installed a small listening device.

The other room where people spent a lot of time was in the kitchen, so he installed one there, too, behind the outlet where the toaster was plugged in. He installed another one in the living room as a backup.

Then he turned on the alarm, left the house, and locked the door, leaving the way he came.

Whatever Shanice's involvement, she wasn't innocent. No one kept that amount of cash on hand for no reason. He just hoped he wasn't a damn fool who had fallen for a sweet act.

SEATED on the lid of the commode in the bathroom at The Bookish Attic, Shanice stared at the number she'd written on a piece of paper. She still didn't know if this was the right decision but had to do something. Spending time with Vicente made her think about her future and the possibilities, and most importantly, she didn't want to risk putting his life in danger. By acting now, she opened the door to a future with him and would keep herself, and him, safe.

This was the right thing to do. Maybe Dennis was wrong. Maybe there was someone she could trust.

She dialed the number for the FBI field office. When they answered, she swallowed hard and launched into an explanation.

"Hello, my name is Shanice, and I'm in possession of some data that I think you would be interested in."

"What kind of data?" the woman on the other end asked.

"I'm not sure. Names and dollar amounts. I don't understand what it all means, but I know it's bad. There are people willing to kill to get this list."

"And you have this information in your possession?"

Shanice paused, not wanting to say too much. "Are you the person that I should be speaking to?"

The woman's voice gentled. "Ma'am, I need to get more information from you so that I'll know how to route your call."

"That's all the information I'm able to give you. The only other thing I can tell you is that someone close to me died because of this information. I don't want to die," she said, voice trembling at the end.

"I understand. Based on what you've told me so far, I believe I know who I should route your call to. Please hold for Agent Stenson."

"Thank you."

Shanice waited in the silence while the call was being transferred. Then she had a thought. What if the agent who came on the line didn't believe her or didn't do anything to help? What if...?

Shanice squeezed her eyes shut, paralyzed by fear. Dennis was dead, and she was pretty sure he hadn't killed himself. Could she be next?

"Hello, this is Agent Stenson."

Shanice opened her mouth to speak, fully intending to tell him everything. Instead, she slammed her mouth shut and hung up the phone.

Shaking, she buried her face in her hands and fought the urge to cry. Not yet. She wasn't ready to divulge what she knew.

That same feeling, the overwhelming sense of aloneness that had consumed her the past couple of months, charged back into her life.

She knew she had to do something. She just didn't know what.

9

The ride home seemed extra long, and Shanice almost kept driving, heading out of town to go far away from her troubles. She wanted to start over. But where would she go?

She pulled onto the street where she lived, surprised there wasn't a single car parked on either side of the road like normal. The tech guy's house was dark.

Because of his constant partying, the neighbors had called the police a few times, so maybe he'd finally settled down and was showing respect to the people who lived here.

Or maybe he's out of town, she thought.

Whatever the reason, tonight she got a break from maneuvering between all of his guests' cars clogging the street.

As she pulled into the driveway, her phone chimed. She fished it out of her bag and saw a text from Ava.

Ava: Don't be mad. I need to cancel. He called and wants us to get together tonight. Can I take a raincheck?

Shanice parked in the garage so she could reply.

Shanice: Of course I'm not mad. Have fun, and the next time I see you, I want all the details.

A twist of jealousy pricked her chest.

Ava: Deal! [kissy face]

Maybe she should call Vicente.

No. Stop being needy. She wanted company, but tonight was a night for thinking and planning. She considered trying the FBI field office again but wasn't sure if she should. Maybe she should simply walk in there and tell them everything she knew.

Shanice let out a loud cry of exasperation. She liked to read. She liked walks on the beach and picking fruit in the summer. Her life used to be simple and uneventful. She had no clue how to navigate law enforcement and the information in her possession.

Once inside the house, she stopped suddenly and faced the door leading into the garage. Had she forgotten to turn on the alarm before she left? Sometimes she did forget. This was such a good neighborhood, there were times both she and Beatrice left the house without setting it, especially if they were going somewhere nearby and planned to come back within a short period of time.

Standing in the middle of the kitchen, her skin prickled with unease. She surveyed the room—the sparkling steel appliances and the toaster on the counter to her right. Nothing appeared out of place, yet the house was...off, for lack of a better word. The air, the energy, *something*.

Maybe she *should* call Vicente and beg him to stay with her. She would absolutely feel safer if he was there.

Then she laughed at herself, dismissing her apprehension. She was only nervous because she'd called the FBI office today. The call had reminded her of why she left Texas and the potential danger she faced.

Humming, Shanice poured a glass of water and removed a white plate from the cabinet. She pulled a serrated steak knife from a drawer in the island and cut two thin circles of bread from a loaf in the bread tin. Then she slathered peanut butter and jelly onto the slices and stood eating her snack at the island.

Needing a break from thinking so much, she scrolled through her Twitter feed. She laughed at a funny cat video and then started watching the shenanigans of a YouTube comedian currently trending on Twitter.

Behind her, the pantry door creaked open.

She became perfectly still. Before she could turn around, cold metal pressed into the back of her head, and she heard a click.

Shanice stopped breathing, and she became rigid with fear. *Oh dear god,* that's why the house had felt off. Someone had been inside.

She whimpered, too afraid to move even a millimeter.

"Shh, you're going to be fine. You have something I need," a male voice said.

"I-I don't know what you mean."

She started trembling, eyes sweeping the kitchen for a weapon. She couldn't move fast enough to smash the glass of water over his head. He'd shoot her before her hand lifted halfway from the counter. She could stab him, but how would she get to the serrated knife almost within reach without him shooting her first?

"Don't play dumb, sweetheart."

"If you tell me what you're looking for..." Her voice shook. Maybe she could buy some time until she figured out what to do. He needed something from her and therefore wouldn't kill her right away, right?

"Put the phone down and turn around. Slowly."

"I don't want to see your face." He'd definitely kill her if she saw his face and could identify him.

"Turn the fuck around!" the man said in a harsh tone.

On the verge of tears, Shanice closed her eyes, and her face crumbled.

With a trembling hand, she placed the phone on the island and slowly turned to face the intruder. He was tall and dressed in all black—black jeans and a black T-shirt that showed off his wiry, muscular arms. His dark hair was curly and tapered in the back. With his serious face and cold eyes, he looked like he'd never smiled a day in his life.

He kept the gun pointed only inches from her forehead, which magnified her fear tenfold. What if the gun accidentally went off and he shot her?

At such a devastating thought, Shanice whimpered again and closed her eyes. Terror sent another shiver tearing through her body.

"Shh. You're going to be okay."

"You're going to kill me," she whispered.

"No, I won't. Open your eyes."

Reluctantly, she opened her eyes. If he'd told her to hop on one foot, she would have.

"Back up, slowly."

Shanice backed up, slowly.

The intruder edged forward, as well. Without taking his eyes off her, he picked up her phone and powered it off. He dropped it into his pocket.

"Now it's just you and me, and no chance you'll be able to call anyone, okay? You're not going to try anything funny, are you?"

Shanice shook her head.

"Good girl. Now, tell me where that list is."

"I'm sorry, I don't—"

"Don't bullshit me!" he snarled, anger contorting his face into a mask of reddened fury. "You have a list of names and dollar figures. That's what you said. I need that list. Now."

He knows I called the FBI office.

"I don't know what you mean. You have the wrong person."

"Listen, bitch, I'm being nice, but I'm not going to ask you again."

The words had hardly left his mouth when Vicente entered the kitchen behind him. No glasses. No tie. Wearing a dress shirt and jeans. She had no idea how a man so large had managed to move so quietly.

Shanice blinked in shock. "Vicente," she said, without thinking.

The intruder swung toward him, and Vicente hit his wrist sideways, knocking the pistol from his hand. It flew to the floor, sliding across the tile into a corner.

With an animalistic growl, both men charged at each other, and Shanice jumped back.

Vicente was fast, dodging a fist and following quickly with a blow to the man's neck. He followed that with a powerful fist to the belly.

The man grunted and doubled over, and Vincente grabbed a handful of his hair and slammed his face into the top of the island.

Shanice winced and covered her eyes.

He slammed his head again and again. When he was practically limp with blood leaking from his nose, Vicente grabbed his neck and head and twisted. She heard a crack and the man in black collapsed to the floor at his feet.

Her mouth fell open. "Oh my god! Did you kill him?"

"We need to get out of here. There will be others."

"Others? Do you know him? What are you talking about?"

He looked so different. His eyes seemed darker and more piercing and his jawline firmer. Visually he was the same person, but now he appeared more in control and had an edge.

She backed up some more. "Where did you come from?"

"I'll explain everything when we—"

A man in black crashed through the French doors. Shanice

screamed and turned away from the glass that spewed through the room.

The newcomer, a blond with a buzz cut, lunged for the knife on the island. With amazing agility for a man his size, Vicente swung his body onto the island as the man swiped it up. He slid across the top and slammed his foot into the intruder's chest, forcing him backward. Vicente followed, knocking his back into the edge of the counter and quickly following up with a series of jabs.

The blond swung the knife, but Vicente blocked the swipe with one meaty forearm while ripping the toaster out of the wall. He smashed it across the intruder's head, eliciting a groan of pain, but the man didn't go down. He fought back valiantly, swinging the knife in a wide arc.

But he was outmatched. Vicente was big, strong, and in control. He hopped back from the blade each time his opponent swung and, when he'd evaded the third swipe of the blade, followed up with a swift kick to the other man's torso that sent him careening onto his back.

The knife clattered to the floor out of reach.

They stared at each other, two warriors contemplating the next move. Then Vicente grabbed the white plate from the island and smashed it on the edge of the counter. He swiped up a piece of porcelain as the man scrambled on his hands and knees for the gun in the corner.

The whole time she'd kept her eyes on them, Shanice edged toward the doorway, stepping over the dead body on the floor. She picked up her phone, which had fallen out of his pocket, and tucked it between her breasts as Vicente jumped on the man's back and slit his throat with the jagged edge of the plate.

He snatched up the gun and rolled onto his back, gripping the black weapon in both hands. "Duck!" he yelled.

Shanice dropped low as the sound of bullets powered through the kitchen and shattered glass remnants that hung on the door. Vicente fired three shots over her head in quick succession, and Shanice slammed her hands over her ears to reduce the deafening noise.

Looking over her shoulder, she saw another man in black appeared upright, as if suspended by ropes, his eyes lifeless. Blood pooled like a dark cloud on his black shirt before he dropped dead.

Vicente jumped up right away and checked the magazine of the gun. Seeming satisfied, he stuck it in the back waistband of his jeans.

His dark eyes settled on her and he helped her up. "We need to get out of here. You have two minutes to go upstairs and get whatever you can."

"What's going on? I don't understand what's happening." She trembled with fear and shock.

"Not now," he said tersely. "Go upstairs and get your go bag."

"How do you know—"

He smoothly spun them into the still open pantry as a shot blasted by her ear and shattered another piece of glass dangling on the broken French door.

Holy crap. Someone else had entered the house.

"Stay here," Vincente commanded in a grim voice.

She didn't have to be told twice.

He dropped low and darted out of the pantry, slamming the door behind him.

Shots rang out and Shanice backed as far as she could into the small space. Metal shelves pressed into her shoulders, spine, and buttocks as loud bangs filled the air.

It sounded like a war was taking place out there. Shaking uncontrollably, she heard loud whimpers and realized that was her.

"Calm down. Calm down."

A thump against the door made her jump. Then there was

another. Then the only sounds were the grunts of the men as they fought.

With only a sliver of light coming from under the door, Shanice searched the interior for a weapon. She grabbed a can of kidney beans and prayed she'd never have to use it.

Wait a minute, she had her phone. She didn't doubt that a neighbor had already called the police because of all the gunshots. Hopefully they would be there soon and this nightmare would be over.

She took the phone from between her breasts, freezing when she heard a crash and a loud cry of pain. The sound was so gut-wrenching, her knees gave out and she collapsed into a crouch in the dark space. That wasn't Vicente, was it?

Eyes squeezed tight, she prayed harder than she'd ever prayed before. If God got her out of this mess, she promised to start going back to church the way she'd been raised. She would turn over a new leaf.

Still gripping the can in one hand, she used the other to press the power button and turn on the phone. As the phone powered on, the door sprang open and her head snapped up. She hoisted the can in the air, ready for battle and whatever her fate might be.

Vicente's gaze flicked to the can she held. His shirt was torn open to reveal a fitted white T-shirt underneath, and one sleeve of the dress shirt had been torn and hung loosely halfway to his biceps. Blood spatter was on his hand, shirt, and pants.

"So much blood," she whispered.

"It's not mine." Vicente extended a hand. "We don't have much time. Let's go."

10

Shanice didn't know if Vicente followed her upstairs to keep an eye on her or protect her in case another intruder burst through the door. Whatever the reason, she was glad for him shadowing her because there were five dead men in the house. Somehow he'd managed to kill them all—the last two at the same time, apparently—and remained unscathed, with only a torn shirt and blood stains that weren't his. To think, she'd been concerned about putting *his* life in danger!

She yanked the suitcase to the floor and grabbed her backpack on the top shelf of the closet. When she stepped out, Vicente stood to the side of the window, the blinds inched open so he could look out onto the street below.

Shanice rushed into the bathroom and tossed toiletries into her bag. She was still shaking, but not as badly as before, and her mind was going a million miles per minute.

First of all, she didn't know this man. The way he fought those intruders, he'd done that many times before. Who was he? Who were those men that he killed? Could she trust him? What if he killed her, too?

Back in the bedroom, Vicente turned around to face her. "Time to go." He ripped off the shirt and tossed it to the floor.

Shanice gulped at the size of his biceps. He was *huge.* "Go where?" she asked, voice trembling way more than she'd anticipated. She lifted the backpack onto her shoulder.

"I'll explain later."

He left the room, and she had no choice but to follow. He took the stairs slowly, cautiously, the gun now in his outstretched right hand. She followed close behind him and covered her mouth, the contents of her stomach almost coming up at the smell of discharged bullets and the stench of blood and death in the air. They crept down the stairs, her shaky knees practically useless but holding up. Thank goodness for the wall beside her. She leaned into it for support.

Vicente reached for the door but stopped. "Where's your phone?" he asked.

"In my backpack."

"Give it to me." He held out his hand.

She hesitated.

"Give it to me!" The firmness in his voice didn't allow for arguing.

She took out the phone and handed it over. Vicente removed the SIM card and tossed the phone against the far wall, like it was trash.

"My phone!"

He then crushed the SIM card with the heel of his shoe.

"What are you doing?"

He ignored her protests and opened the door, scanning the area before motioning for her to follow. As they moved down the walkway, Shanice's eyes darted around the neighborhood. A neighbor across the street was peeping around the curtains.

Vicente stopped suddenly, and she bumped into him from behind. The man was pure muscle—hard and coiled muscle. He was staring at the house across the street—the one where the tech guy lived. The front door was wide open and all the windows dark. It looked eerily empty.

"Hurry," he said.

Shanice scrambled into the car and Vicente rushed around to the driver side. This wasn't the gray Nissan he'd brought her home in. This was a black, older model Ford Mustang and better fit this man who had fought off a series of assailants.

He slotted the gun into a black metal holster mounted below the steering column, and the magnetic pull snapped the weapon into place. With the barrel pointed at the floor, it would be easy for him to yank out the gun and start firing if necessary.

"Hang on."

Shanice gripped the roof handle as he pressed the accelerator to the floor. He swung a hard left into the street, tires squealing as the tread skidded on the road's surface to gain traction. Suddenly, a shot cracked through the air, and the back passenger window disintegrated into pieces. Shanice cried out and ducked. Shards of glass scattered across the back seat and nicked the arm holding onto the handle. From the corner of her eye, she saw a man dressed in all black come running from the house.

"Get down!" Vicente growled.

He grabbed her neck and pushed her lower in the car. Whimpering, Shanice squeezed her eyes shut. The shivers started again, fear beating relentlessly in her skull and causing crippling terror and anxiety.

Police sirens sounded in the distance. She was partially relieved, but how the hell would they explain everything that had happened here tonight?

Five dead men, Beatrice's house wrecked and riddled with bullet holes, and broken glass all over the kitchen floor. Now this—more gunshots in the middle of the street!

Vicente slammed on the brakes, and her head lightly

bumped the glove compartment. Opening one eye, Shanice saw him glare at the rear-view mirror. The shots had stopped.

What was he doing? They could get away. All he had to do was drive. Vicente shoved the gear into reverse and propelled the car backward.

Shanice shut her eye again. *No, no, no.*

More shots rang out. Vicente propelled the vehicle backward at a breakneck speed. She felt a right turn and then...*thump.* The Mustang hit something—or rather, someone. The man must have tried to get out of the way, but Vicente turned and hit him anyway.

She heard the body roll over the top and down across the hood. Vicente slammed on the brakes again, and they jerked to a stop.

"Hang on."

He pulled off and ran over the man a second time! The car bounced over the body in a bumpy ride, like traveling over rough, unpaved terrain.

"Oh my god," she squeaked.

Once again on the smooth surface of the street, Shanice slowly lifted her head. The sirens were coming closer, from the west. Vicente drove faster and hung a hard left, going east. They careened away from the approaching police and headed in the opposite direction.

Shanice gripped the door handle so hard her fingers ached. She glanced at the man beside her. He seemed bigger now with the torn off sleeves and exposed muscle, and clearly a killing machine.

She swallowed hard but remained silent as they drove through the streets. He slowed down when they hit the highway and drove more in line with the rest of the cars. No doubt to keep from attracting too much attention. After a few minutes, they pulled into the parking lot of a supermarket.

"I'll be right back."

Shanice simply nodded. Where the hell was she going to go? She was scared shitless. If he hadn't shown up, she could have died tonight. But was she safe with him?

She watched him walk away, his steps more self-assured than the man she'd originally met. His voice was different, too. He not only sounded more confident, his voice was deeper. *Everything about him had been fake.*

Vicente pulled up beside her in another car, a black Toyota sedan.

He got out and yanked open her door. "Get in."

Too numb to do anything but exactly what he said, Shanice clutched her backpack to her chest and climbed into the passenger side of the car. She sank into the soft gray seat and inhaled deeply of the pine air freshener hanging from the rear-view mirror. The car seemed completely normal, and she could almost be lulled into believing that what she'd experienced tonight was not so bad and stealing someone else's transportation was an excusable offense, considering they were on the run from killers. But her mind couldn't quite make the leap, no matter how comfy the seats or normal the scent of air freshener in the vehicle.

Vicente took items from inside the Mustang and dumped them into a duffle bag he pulled from the trunk. He swapped the license plates, tossed the bag into the back seat of the Toyota, and climbed behind the steering wheel. Then they were off.

Knots tortured Shanice's stomach. She didn't know what to think. What the hell was happening?

She shrank against the door, clutching the backpack to her bosom. Outside the window, Miami went by in a stream of cars and lights.

Yesterday she'd eaten dinner in a fine dining restaurant and kissed this man outside her house—her body still tingling long after he'd left and she lay in bed alone. Their budding relationship had seemed so romantic and wonderful, but now she imagined the worst.

To think, she'd fantasized about having sex with this man, after meeting him ten days ago and going on one date.

"Who are you?" she whispered.

He glanced at her but didn't respond.

"You're not an accountant...are you?"

He briefly looked at her again, the lights of oncoming vehicles trailing across his crooked nose and high cheekbones. He still didn't answer the question. He simply returned his gaze to the road.

Shanice hugged herself and prayed that everything would be okay.

Who was Vicente Diaz, and what had she gotten herself into this time?

11

"Y ou'll be safe here."

Cruz dropped his duffle bag and other items on the floor and locked the door from the inside using a key. They'd dumped the car a couple of blocks back and walked to this studio apartment in North Miami, on the second floor of a mostly empty three-story building. A king bed dominated much of the space, and there was a kitchenette, and a blinds-covered window that looked onto the alley below let in a little light.

The apartment was smaller and darker than the place Miles had set up under the Vicente alias. Cruz hadn't been here in a long time, but he liked the neighborhood because it was in a high-crime area where everyone minded their own business.

Shanice stared at him from the doorway, backpack on her shoulder and arms crossed over her torso in a protective gesture. He knew she must have a slew of questions to ask.

"Are you going to explain what's going on?" she asked.

"Yes, but you need to sit down first."

"I don't need to sit down first! Who are you?" she demanded. "Because there's no way the average accountant has the ability to kill a bunch of men, steal a car, and have a secret hideout in one of the roughest neighborhoods in the city."

Even with the scared expression on her face, she was still a beautiful woman.

"If I didn't kill them, they would have killed you."

"And how exactly did you know I was in danger? How did you know to show up?"

He hesitated, knowing she wouldn't like the answer. "I planted listening devices in your home. I'd followed you from work and was nearby and listening when I heard you were in trouble."

Her eyes opened to the size of dinner plates. "*What?* You were *spying* on me? What the hell is going on!" She was shaking, on the verge of hyperventilating.

He took a cautious step toward her. "Shanice, calm down."

"I will *not* calm down."

She started breathing very fast. With the adrenaline gone, the stress of the past hour was hitting her. She dropped the backpack to the floor and clutched her chest.

Vicente rushed over, and she lifted a hand to fend him off, but he scooped her up in his arms and strode over to the bed. He set her down and crouched before her.

"Cup your hands and breathe into them. Slowly... Yes, like that."

She repeated the breathing technique, and after a couple of minutes her breathing was back to normal.

He looked into her eyes. "You don't have to be afraid of me."

"You've been spying on me, and after what I saw tonight, I'm not so sure." She swallowed. "What do you want?"

"What makes you think I want something?"

She laughed bitterly. "Because the first man you killed wanted something, and if you were listening, I have to assume you want the same thing. I'm sure you heard him."

"I did. Do you have it?"

"Have what?"

"The data."

"If you were listening, you heard my answer." She stared angrily at him then ducked her gaze.

"This isn't a game, Shanice," Vicente said with a thread of steel in his voice. "It's a matter of national security. People's lives are at risk."

She looked at him again. "Who are you? FBI?"

"No, but I can't tell you who I'm working for."

"Well, I don't know anything about any data," she snapped.

"We both know that's not true."

"No, we don't. I—" She paused, a frown wrinkling her brow. "Wait a minute, is that why you started dating me?"

Cruz didn't reply.

Her mouth fell open. "I'm right, aren't I? You asked me out, pretended to like me, even kissed me, because you thought I had something you wanted. How far were you going to go? Were you going to fuck me, too?"

Her lower lip trembled and the hurt in her eyes indicted him for his dishonesty. *Mierda.*

Jaw tightening, she lifted her head higher. "Well you wasted your precious time taking me to dinner and pretending to like poetry to get close to me. All that work, and you'll have nothing to show for your fake attention."

He'd enjoyed talking books and poetry with her on their only date. None of that had been fake. Neither had his feelings been fake. He did like her and he liked kissing her —a lot.

"I wasn't faking."

Eyes blazing with fury, she pointed a finger in his face. "Don't you dare pretend that you felt anything more than you did. You're a liar and a fraud. Your name isn't even Vicente, is it? Everything has been a lie. You wanted something from me and did whatever you needed to, to get it. And I was too foolish to figure it out. Goodness, you're good. Well, I'm sorry to disappoint you, but I don't have what you're looking for."

Underneath the anger, he heard the pain his ruse had caused. Despite what she believed, he had never meant to hurt her. But this was not the time to get sentimental. He had a mission to accomplish, and love and affection did not go hand-in-hand with death and espionage.

"I'm not the only one lying."

"I am not lying!" She jumped up from the bed. "I don't know anything. Can I go now?"

He stood too, towering over her. "No."

"I'll scream."

"Scream all you want. No one will hear you, and if they did, they wouldn't care." He decided to try another tactic. "It's late, and you've been through a lot. We should get some sleep and talk in the morning."

"I'm not tired."

"Well, I am. Killing all those men took a lot out of me," he said sarcastically.

Her eyes traveled over him, taking in the blood-spattered white shirt and the blood on his hands. He suffered some bruises and had gotten a few nicks from rolling in glass, but otherwise he was in good shape. Nothing a few hours' rest wouldn't fix.

"There's only one bed," she said in a thick voice.

"That's right. We'll be sharing it."

"I'm not sharing a bed with you."

He shrugged. "You can sleep on the floor, if you like. Or sit up all night in that chair." He pointed to the rolling chair pushed under the desk against the wall.

"I'm the guest. You should let me have the bed."

"Not tonight, *mami*."

Sharing a bed with her was not his best idea. He'd probably be hard as a rock within minutes of lying next to her, but that was the only option tonight because he intended to get a good night's rest, on a mattress.

She hugged herself and watched as he took an extra pillow from the closet and kicked off his shoes.

"I have to pee," she announced.

Vicente pointed to the right of the bed. "Bathroom is through that door."

"I want to take a shower, too. I feel...icky. I always take a shower at night. But you probably already know that, since you've been spying on me."

He was two seconds away from throttling her. He shot her a tight smile. "There's soap and towels in the bathroom."

Shanice picked up her backpack.

"Where are you going with that?" Vicente asked.

"My toothbrush and toiletries are in here." She walked toward the bathroom.

"Don't take forever. I need to wash up, too."

She closed the door and he heard the lock engage.

SHANICE RESTED her forehead against the door. What a freaking night! Vicente wasn't who he said he was, and someone had sent a team to kill her. How did they find her? Was it possible she couldn't even trust the FBI?

She closed her eyes and took a deep, calming breath.

Now she was in an even worse situation than before because she didn't have a phone or a safe home. Being with Vicente didn't make her feel truly safe because she didn't know him. She cringed as she remembered last night's kiss and how much she'd ached for him to make love to her. What a fool she'd been.

She needed to bide her time until the right moment to get away because she didn't trust him. He knew about the list and said he wasn't FBI, yet he couldn't tell her who he worked for. Well, that wasn't good enough.

She turned away from the door and examined the interior of the bathroom. It was small, with a frosted window next to the commode. Wondering if it led to the alley they accessed to enter the building, she pushed to lift it up. Fortunately, it wasn't painted shut. It squeaked a little bit, so she raised it up very slowly to limit the noise. At the same time, she listened for movement from Vicente.

Standing on tiptoe, she peered out. The alley was right there, one floor below, and a main street ran perpendicular to it. In the dim light, she saw a dumpster, and if she landed on that, the drop wouldn't be too bad. Then she could get away. This might be her way out.

With a burst of excitement, Shanice grabbed her backpack.

Vicente rapped on the door and she jumped. "Are you all right in there?" he called.

"Yes, I'm fine. Can I have a little time alone, please?"

"Just checking on you."

"I'm about to get in the shower."

She turned on the water and then climbed onto the lid of the toilet. With her backpack over one arm, since she couldn't put it on her back if she wanted to fit through the window, she hoisted herself up.

She didn't have a whole lot of time and didn't want to be in there too long because Vicente would become suspicious. She climbed out and onto the ledge created from a joint where Vicente's apartment connected with the one below. Very carefully, keeping her chest pressed to the dirty brick wall, Shanice shifted the bag onto her back and prepared for the next step. She had to be very, very careful.

Balancing precariously, she lay flat on the narrow ledge and then slid sideways so her feet dangled over the edge.

Don't look down. Don't look down, she told herself repeatedly.

With a quick prayer in the hope she wouldn't injure herself, she shifted the rest of her body over the ledge. Unfortunately, she didn't have the upper body strength needed to hold on. Her fingers slipped and she grappled not to lose her grip. With a small cry, she dropped onto the dumpster with a loud thump.

Out of breath, on her sore bottom, and with bruised fingertips, she wiggled her hands and feet and realized she hadn't been badly hurt. Her pride had taken the worst beating.

Grinning, she looked up at the window and shook her head. One of these days, she'd go back to her normal, easy-going life. Until then, she had to find a new hiding place and figure out what to do next.

Shanice climbed off the dumpster and dusted off her clothes. With a brisk walk, she took off for the street that crossed the alley...and came to an abrupt halt. Fear jumped into her throat.

Vicente stood in the doorway where they'd entered earlier. He looked completely at ease, arms crossed over his massive chest, umber eyes flinty and filled with accusation.

"Going somewhere?" he asked.

12

H is grip on her upper arm was tight and angry as he dragged her up the stairs.

"You're hurting me," Shanice said.

In response, Vicente muttered a stream of Spanish words, which she was pretty sure were curse words. At the apartment door, he pushed her inside and she stumbled forward.

He locked the door and stalked toward her. "What the hell were you thinking? Why did you run? You could have seriously hurt yourself climbing out that window. "

"I was scared! I wanted to get away from you. I don't know who you are!" She'd seen what he'd done to those men and didn't want him to do the same to her.

"I'm the guy who saved your ass less than two hours ago."

"Maybe you did that so you could kill me later if I give you the data you say you need."

"If I wanted to kill you, I'd have already done it. If I wanted to get the information out of you, which I know you're lying about, there are ways to do that, *believe* me."

The veiled threat did nothing to put her mind at ease.

"You think running away from me is a good idea? How long

will you keep running, eh? They killed your neighbor across the street and took over his house to get to you. They're going to keep coming for you, and when they can't get to you, they'll move on to your family members. They might go after your mother. Is that what you want?"

"No! Don't say that."

"They've killed once before. There's nothing to stop them from killing again because they haven't gotten what they wanted."

"I want to go back to normal. I want to feel safe again."

"You can't go back to normal. Normal is done for you," Vicente said in a grim tone. "Enough of this bullshit. Your boyfriend stole some information—information that if it gets out could jeopardize our national security."

"I don't have a boyfriend."

"Your ex-boyfriend, then."

"My ex-boyfriend had nothing to do with this." What he was saying didn't make any sense.

"He had everything to do with this! He told his wife that he was working on a big exposé, something huge. He claimed to have seen a pattern in the data he stole."

She blinked, utterly confused. "Wait a minute, are you talking about Dennis?"

"Yes, Dennis. Your married ex." He said the words with biting distaste.

"You think I was having an affair with Dennis? No! We weren't lovers. We were friends."

"Friends who have sleepovers?" he asked snidely.

"What are you talking about...? Oh...no, he stayed over at my place one time, and that was because he'd had too much to drink. The same night he told me about the...data."

His eyes narrowed with suspicion. "So you admit you know about it."

"Yes," Shanice replied in a small voice. Suddenly very tired, she placed the backpack on the floor and sat on the edge of the bed. "Instead of driving home, I told him to sleep on my couch."

"He could have called a Lyft or a cab," Cruz said pointedly.

"Why spend money when I had an available couch and he was my *friend*?"

Cruz examined her, searching for the lies in her statement. She didn't flinch or avert her eyes. This time she was telling the truth, and she wanted to make that clear. There was no romantic relationship between her and Dennis.

Cruz dragged the rolling chair in front of her and sat down. "Tell me everything."

"Before I do, will you tell me something?"

"What?"

"What's your name?"

"Vicente," he said in a clipped voice.

"No, your real name. Not the one you made up to get close to me and make a fool out of me."

"I didn't make a fool out of you."

"So you were genuinely planning to pursue a relationship with me?"

She didn't know why she kept pushing him—why she kept wanting him to say that she was wrong and that he really did care for her. Was it simply because she cared about him? She couldn't get rid of the sour taste of betrayal, no matter how much she tried.

He sighed, rubbing the back of his neck. "You're a difficult woman. Before I tell you my name, I need to know you won't try to run again. You need to decide now. Are you going to take your chances on your own, or take your chances and stay with me? What's it going to be?"

She hesitated, but in retrospect didn't have much of a choice. "I'll stay with you," she answered in a low voice.

Her actions had been impulsive, and the thought of endangering her mother had never crossed her mind. He studied her for long moments, and she waited with tight insides.

Finally, he responded. "Cruz. My name is Cruz, and that's all I can tell you for now. You have to trust me, because I'm your only hope."

She didn't know if what he'd told her was true, but she had no choice but to believe him at this point. Even if he didn't have genuine romantic feelings toward her, he did have a point, that he'd saved her life tonight.

"Okay. Cruz." Trying out his name, she decided she liked it. "I need to explain my relationship with Dennis, because you have it all wrong. We were not lovers. We were always only friends. We went to high school together and lost touch but ran into each other at a bookstore a few years ago and developed a friendship. At the time, he was going through a rough patch with his wife and things weren't getting any better. I happened to be going through a rough patch with my boyfriend at the time—that's who I thought you were talking about. We comforted each other, that's it. He listened to me complain, and I listened to him complain. We gave each other advice. A true, genuine, trusting friendship developed from that."

She stopped for a moment, watching him to make sure he didn't doubt her words. She couldn't tell whether or not he believed her because his face didn't give anything away.

"Continue. How did he end up with the data?"

"It was all part of an investigation he was working on. Whenever he was working on something big, he tended to be very secretive about it, so he wouldn't give me much information, except to say that it was a big deal. The night he stayed at my apartment, he told me more. He had a list of names, but he never said anything about national security. What he did tell me was that Logan Investors was under investigation for questionable practices in real estate development."

Cruz leaned forward, resting his elbows on his knees. "Who the hell is Logan Investors?"

"They're based out of Houston, but they have developments all over the country—condominiums, apartment complexes, and commercial space. The Logans are stinking rich. Billionaires. The owner and head of the company is Randall Logan and he has all kinds of political connections. He's like a god in Houston. Dennis was working on something huge regarding him. The only problem is, I think they must have found out and picked him up."

"Who picked him up?" Cruz asked. His eyebrows had formed a deep vee as he listened.

"The police. They grabbed him at home, at the apartment he was renting. They accused him of using cocaine. And yes, he had a drug problem in the past, but he'd been clean for a long time and wouldn't have started using again."

"You don't know that. People slip up and go back to rehab."

"We were close—best friends. I knew him, and I would have known if he was using again. He was fine. Better than fine. He was even optimistic that things would work out between him and his wife, and they were talking about getting back together."

"She mentioned that," Cruz said slowly.

"See? He wouldn't screw that up, because he looked forward to having his family back. Plus he was busy with this investigation and mentioned more than once that this could be his shot at a Pulitzer. This exposé was his big break, a way to prove that he was worthy of being with the niece of Senator Sandoval. He called me from jail and told me not to come down there because he didn't want me to get involved. He said the cops planted the drugs in his apartment, claiming they'd received a tip."

"So you're saying that Randall Logan had the police in his back pocket and got them to arrest Dennis?"

Shanice nodded. "That's exactly what I'm telling you. Dennis was scared, and before he went to jail he told me about his concerns. He told me not to trust anyone with the information he'd given me."

"So he gave you the names?"

"Yes, he did. But before I left Texas, someone broke into my apartment. Dennis was old school and used notebooks all the time. He had a separate one with that list of names and asked me to hide it for him, as insurance in case something happened to him. But when they broke into my apartment, they found the notebook in the hiding place and took it."

"If they took the notebook, then why were they after you tonight?"

"Maybe because I called the FBI earlier today, after you and I talked."

"What did you tell them?"

"I told them that I had the list. But I got scared at the last minute and hung up when one of the agents came on the phone."

Cruz straightened in the chair. "What you're saying doesn't make sense. Why would you tell them you had the list when you just told me the notebook was stolen from your apartment?"

Shanice fisted her hands in her lap and stared at her clenched fingers. This was it. The moment of truth. "Because I made a copy." She looked up at him.

"Where is it?"

She tapped her right temple. "Here."

13

Cruz looked understandably confused. "What do you mean...?"

"The information is all in my head. The names and the dollar amounts next to them."

"What were the dollar amounts for?"

Shanice shrugged. "Bribes, maybe? Dennis wrote down each name and a dollar amount next to it. He didn't tell me what the numbers meant, but I assumed they were bribes."

"And you memorized all of that? How?"

"Like I told you, my father was a cognitive psychologist," Shanice replied with another shrug. "He studied the capabilities of the human brain and our capacity to retain information. He believed we could increase that capacity through brain exercises. One of the studies he conducted was how to reduce the risk of dementia. He taught me the same memorization techniques he used with his patients, and the more I did them, the better I became. I trained my brain, the way a runner trains for a marathon or an athlete for a triathlon."

"That's incredible. You never forget anything?"

"No, nothing quite so amazing," Shanice said with a short laugh. "But if I study to remember, I can remember. Lists are really easy to memorize, and the information in the notebook was one long list."

"We have to get that information to the authorities."

"To who? Dennis told me not to trust anyone, and I've been sitting on this information for two months, unsure what to do. Then I call the FBI field office, and *the same day*, someone is in my house holding a gun to my head."

"Which means they either bugged your phone or they have a contact at the field office."

"I've never left my phone unattended. I always have it with me. Which means..."

"There are other ways to intercept your phone calls, but I've kept a close watch on you since I arrived in Miami, and I would have noticed if you were being tailed. That could only mean one thing—Logan has someone at the FBI office, which means we can't trust them, either."

He'd said what she'd been worried about, and Shanice became overwhelmed by fear. "Dennis warned me. How could I have been so stupid?" she said shakily.

"Don't be so hard on yourself. It's natural to expect law enforcement to protect us, but they don't always."

"No kidding."

"There's one more question I have to ask you. You have almost fifty thousand dollars in that backpack. I know, because I entered your house today when you were at work and searched every room for the notebook."

"You're really making me feel at ease about your behavior."

"Believe me, I'm one of the good guys. Where'd you get the money, Shanice?"

"My father, from his insurance policy when he died three years ago. That's what's left of my half of one hundred thousand dollars. My mother got the other half. Before I left Texas, I withdrew all of my money, sold my car, and gave away or sold most of my personal items. I wanted to pay cash for everything so I couldn't get tracked."

A hint of admiration entered his eyes. "Good girl."

Her cheeks warmed at the compliment. "There's something else I should tell you that I completely forgot about. Dennis had a storage unit where I think he might have kept some personal items. I don't know what exactly, but I'd forgotten about it because he only mentioned the unit in passing once. I don't know where it is, but I figure it's in or near Houston."

"Excellent. Anything else you can think of?"

Shanice fell silent, searching the crevices of her mind for other clues or tidbits of information she could share with Cruz. "No, nothing."

"Okay," he said with a nod. "You did good. Thank you for sharing that information with me."

"What happens now?"

"You go take a shower. A real one, this time." He arched an eyebrow and her cheeks reddened. "I'll make a call. There's someone who can help, who's not connected to the FBI."

"Who?"

"My direct supervisor at the agency I work for. Let me handle this part."

"But what if he's involved?"

"He's not, I promise you. But I won't divulge more information than I have to."

He must have seen the fear in her eyes, because he edged the chair closer and cupped her left cheek with a warm palm. "I won't let anything happen to you. I promise. Do you believe me?"

Looking into his eyes at close range, she didn't doubt for one second that he would do whatever he needed to do to protect her. She was confident Cruz would act as a barrier between her and the people trying to do her physical harm. Cruz was vastly different from Vicente. Vicente was nice and sweet. This man—this man was dangerous. With him on her side, the enemy didn't stand a chance.

"I believe you," she whispered.

"Good." His thumb brushed her cheek, and she leaned into his hand, closing her eyes in relief. She was no longer alone and didn't have to carry the burden of what Dennis had shared with her by herself.

When she opened her eyes again, Cruz was looking at her in a different way. His eyes had lowered to her lips, and her breath hitched. Their eyes met, and the tension in the room kicked up to a scorching level.

As she continued to look at him, his expression became shuttered and he jerked back as if she'd burned him, squashing the moment of tension. Yet she continued to feel the burden of the heat between them even after he stood abruptly and shoved the chair under the desk.

He walked over to the closet and pulled out a white T-shirt that was folded on top of a shelf. He handed the garment to her without making eye contact. "You can sleep in this. Go take your shower, and I'll make my call."

Shanice took the soft cotton shirt and picked up her backpack. She carried everything into the bathroom and didn't lock the door this time, instead leaning back against it.

The events of the night had been a temporary distraction, but nothing had changed—she still wanted him, more now that this very capable, in-control man had emerged.

Who was going to protect her against him—and what he would assuredly do to her heart?

WHAT THE HELL was wrong with him?

He'd completed this type of assignment many times before. Get close, find out what she knows, and complete the mission. Not so easy this time around. Shanice was in his blood, under his skin.

Aggravated, Cruz tended to his cuts with the first-aid kit he had stashed under the kitchen sink. He dabbed alcohol on the sliced skin on his neck and shoulder and placed a Band-Aid on the busted knuckle of his right hand.

Then he set about to do what he promised. Reaching under the desk, he yanked on the encrypted phone he had taped to the bottom. Making a call to another encrypted phone meant no one could listen in or intercept the conversation.

He powered on the device and started dialing. He had to get a message to Miles and let him know what was going on. The mission he'd been sent to perform was not exactly what they thought it was. He was almost done dialing the number when he paused, thumb hovering over the eighth digit.

Something wasn't right. What did the list of names mean?

He doubted they had anything to do with national security. Maybe instead of turning Shanice over to Miles or anyone else, he could do a little investigating of his own. He asked her to trust him, so now he had to display the same level of trust. He needed to make a decision—complete the mission by handing her over with everything she knew, or dig a little deeper to get to the bottom of this mystery?

He already knew what his decision would be. He needed to dig a little deeper.

In a short time, he'd come to care for Shanice, and he would never forgive himself if anything happened to her.

He cleared the numbers and hoped he wasn't letting his feelings cloud his judgment. Instead, he dialed the number of a friend he could trust. Listening to the phone ring, he cast a glance at the dark alley below. Nothing untoward, no suspicious activity. He was fairly certain they hadn't been followed, but one could never be too careful.

"Yo, Cruz, what's up, man?"

Cruz grinned at the sound of his friend's voice. Some agents, like him and Raheem, had developed relationships over the years that turned into true friendships and they kept in touch. For many of them, the Plan B agents were the only family they had. The benefit was, whenever they needed help with an operation off the books, they had someone to call.

"*¿Que bola, acere?* How have you been? What are you up to?" he asked.

"Shit."

Cruz chuckled. "I have a job for you. You interested?"

Raheem was what they called an "information specialist." He could access all sorts of information, and given enough time, hack just about any corporation's server. Plan B pulled him into the network after he accessed a tech company's mainframe and sent millions in direct deposits to their employees after learning the CEO was getting a bonus while the employees received layoffs.

He faced up to ten years in prison for computer fraud, wire fraud, and a host of other charges, but Plan B offered him a job, which he gladly accepted at the age of sixteen. He was much older now and even better at accessing difficult-to-access information.

"Hell yeah, I'm bored as hell."

"Good. I'll make sure you have stellar accommodations."

"Last time you promised stellar accommodations, I was sleeping on a sand floor in the middle of the desert."

"I promise you won't experience anything like that. You'll even have a roof over your head. Can you be in Houston tomorrow?"

"Sure can."

"I was hoping you'd say that. Bring all your tools. I'll need you to analyze a list of names. There's a claim that the names on the list have something to do with national security."

"Doesn't sound like you believe that."

"I don't. Here's something you can work on until I see you. I need to find the storage unit for a Dennis Ray, an investigative reporter for the *Houston Times*. He's dead now but was married to Karen Sandoval, Senator Joseph Sandoval's niece."

"Whoa. What have you gotten yourself into?"

"Hopefully you can help me figure that out. Search everywhere in the Houston area and neighboring cities."

"Consider it done."

After their conversation, Cruz went over to the kitchenette and opened one of the drawers next to the refrigerator. He pulled out a butter knife and then walked over to the far right corner of the apartment. Getting down on his knees, he used the knife to pry up a loose floorboard.

He grabbed a handful of cash and a fake ID. He thumbed through a stack of credit cards and found the one that had the same name as the fake ID. Then he replaced the floorboard.

Tomorrow, they were going to Houston, but to keep Shanice safe, he'd call an old friend to fly them there, which would allow him to hide her identity.

A few minutes later, he was sitting on the chair, contemplating everything that needed to be done the next day, when the bathroom door opened.

Shanice stepped out wearing his T-shirt, and he almost swallowed his tongue. He'd never thought of his shirt as sheer, but he could see her hard nipples and the surrounding dark areolas, and she clearly wasn't wearing any panties. She stood there for a second with the cotton torturing him as it stretched across her hips and bosom.

He gulped.

She smiled faintly and rested her backpack and the clothes she'd been wearing beside the wall. When she bent down, he caught a tantalizing view of the low hemline riding up a little on her round bottom, teasing him by not offering a full glimpse. She was a sexy woman, and his mind ran wild with the possibilities.

She straightened. "The bathroom is all yours."

Great. He'd make full use of it jacking off in the shower.

14

_____

When Cruz exited the bathroom, refreshed from a cool shower and wearing nothing but a pair of plaid boxers, Shanice was already asleep. She must have been exhausted. She'd been through a lot tonight.

Before going into the bathroom, he'd told her about his plan for them to go back to Houston. She'd looked worried, but he reassured her that everything would be fine and she could trust his friend Raheem.

He took a moment to watch her sleep, curled on her side facing the window and under the thin sheet that she'd pulled over her body. Her lashes brushed her full cheeks, and light filtered between the half-open blinds and sliced across her face in a striped pattern of light and dark. Her pink lips lay partially open in sleep, and he wished he could get rid of the gnawing need to taste them again.

She'd washed her underwear and left the black lacy cheeky drying on the towel rack, making his imagination run wild. Sleeping in his shirt, wearing nothing underneath, didn't help. He was so aroused, he considered joining her on the bed, and not to get some rest. He'd insisted on sleeping next to her, but now he wasn't so sure that was a good idea.

Cruz closed the blinds and went to lie on his back on the other side of the mattress. The tantalizing scent of honey and ginger made his blood run hot and tightened his gut. He'd never wanted to sleep with a woman this badly before, and he'd come to the conclusion that it was because he was depriving himself. Normally, he didn't think anything about having sex with a woman during an operation. He compartmentalized his emotions and considered sex a bonus—part of the benefit of doing what he did. But as much as he wanted Shanice, he hesitated, and now that he knew she was on the right side of the law, that made him hold back even more.

Her innocence gnawed at him. He still didn't know why he'd told her his real name. That piece of information was usually kept secret, but he'd wanted her to know. Why?

Maybe because he saw the possibility of what he could have with her. Something real. Something permanent.

What the hell was wrong with him? *Go to sleep, Cruz.*

Thankfully, he did manage to fall asleep but woke up to the sound of quiet whimpers.

It was Shanice. During the night, she'd shifted over to his side of the bed. His vision adjusted to the ambient light, and there was rapid eye movement under her closed lids. She twitched in her sleep and whimpered again.

Her eyes suddenly flew open, and she gasped, staring at him in shock as if she'd forgotten who he was and where they were. Blinking, she focused and the confusion cleared from her eyes.

Cruz rolled onto his side. "Are you okay?" He gently pushed a tangle of curls back from her damp brow.

"I was dreaming about Beatrice and my mother, and..." Her voice shook as tears filled her eyes.

"It's okay, it was only a dream."

"It's not okay. I'll never forgive myself if either of them get hurt."

"That won't happen. I won't let that happen."

"How?"

He considered the question and then answered, "I have some friends who owe me a favor. They have a cabin in the mountains where your mother could stay and will be safe. As for Beatrice, I doubt anyone will bother her now that you're gone. By now, they know the reason you escaped is because of me. They'll be looking for me and you. Beatrice will be safe on her cruise and will be safe when she gets back. If all goes well, we'll have this resolved before she even returns from her trip."

"But her house is trashed. I'm sure she'll want to come back to assess the damage and fix the place. And she'll be worried about me. At the very least I need to let her know that I'm okay."

"Then that's what we'll do, but we'll notify her the safe way."

"What's the safe way?" Shanice asked, sounding a little less worried now that he'd presented a solution.

"Tomorrow we'll buy a burner phone and make a couple of calls to the people you care about, to reassure them that you're okay. But that's the last time you'll be able to talk to them until this is over, is that clear? We can't risk making contact with them on unsecured lines."

"Okay. Thank you," she said gratefully.

"No problem."

In the ensuing silence, her gaze traveled over his naked chest and arms, and she touched the Band-Aid on the back of his hand. "You were hurt."

"Only a scratch."

Her forefinger traced a puckered scar on his chest, near the right shoulder joint. It was over an inch wide and depressed into the skin with what looked like pale threads radiating from it.

"That's not a scratch," she said.

"No, it's not."

"What happened, if you don't mind sharing?"

"Someone got the drop on me five years ago. I let my guard down, and he shot me in the shoulder. The bullet went straight through and out my back. It burned like hell, and I was bleeding all over the place. I promised myself that I'd never allow myself to get shot again. So far so good."

"Wow," she said, sounding impressed. "You know, you were incredible tonight. Do you ever lose a fight?"

He smiled. She was adorable. "I hate pain and hate losing, which made me learn to be better, faster, and smarter than my opponents. That way they never get the upper hand. It's also wise to know when you're outmatched."

Her eyebrows rose in surprise. "I can't imagine you being outmatched by anyone."

He smiled again. "It doesn't happen too often."

"You seem fearless."

"I'm not. But fear doesn't have to be a bad thing. The trick is to manage your fear. Keeps you from being careless, and in my case, usually my instincts kick in to ensure that my fears don't become reality. But a healthy dose of fear is good."

She bit her lush bottom lip. "Can I ask you something else?"

"Sure."

"Do you really enjoy history and poetry?"

His chest warmed with the memory of the dinner conversation on their date. "Yes. I told you, I wasn't being fake with you, and I enjoyed your company. Very much."

Her eyes softened, and he made a decision right then. He no longer wanted to deprive himself of her mouth. The need to kiss her had become an unbearable burden, and he finally gave in to the urge.

Cruz edged closer and Shanice didn't move away. Her lids lowered to half mast, and his lips fastened with confidence over hers, the initial contact sending a charge straight to his groin. And while he'd meant to be gentle, the minute their mouths connected, he lost all reason.

Cruz rolled on top of her, pressing her into the mattress. Hot and unyielding, his lips greedily caressed hers, while the slow grind of his hips between her thighs pulled long moans from the depths of her throat.

He'd forgotten that she was naked under the shirt and shuddered when he fingered her wet cleft. She was already dripping, twisting and pushing up into his stroking fingers with feverishly gyrating hips.

Cruz became as hard as stone. He wanted her so bad he could almost taste it. His hand moved to the back of her head and he deepened the kiss, addicted to the flavor of her mouth. The never-ending liplock tortured as it teased, and she was so responsive, with sensual movements that made it hard for him to think straight.

He pushed two fingers into her wet body while continuing to plunder her mouth. The head of his erection nudged through the split in his boxers, and his balls ached with the need to bury himself inside her.

"*Mami, t'eres un mango,*" he whispered huskily.

She reached into his boxers, the warm clasp of her hand gently stroking his engorged manhood. For a few blissful seconds he reveled in the sensations caused by her soft, delicate fingers on his hard flesh. He groaned past the tightness in his throat, the ache to possess her taking on a life of its own as he thrust his hips against her hand.

One time. He only needed one time to satisfy his blinding lust for her, and then he'd be good. But reason returned like a flash of lightning, and he grabbed her wrist.

Glassy-eyed, she stared up at him in confusion.

"Shanice, we can't."

"What?" Her heaving breaths brushed his lips.

With regret, Cruz rolled onto his back and stared up at the ceiling. He'd gotten carried away. "That was a mistake." Even as he said the words, his hard penis threatened to revolt.

"I'm not sorry that you kissed me," she whispered.

He laughed, albeit painfully. He'd regret this decision when he woke up with sore balls in the morning. His behavior was hard to explain, but he tried anyway. "I shouldn't have kissed you. I don't want to mislead you, Shanice. I can't give you what you want. There's no pursuing a relationship—no future for us. When this is over, I'm gone, and you'll never see me again."

The hunger in her eyes shrank to nothingness. She withdrew from him and tugged down the hem of his T-shirt. "Thanks for the warning."

"This isn't a rejection of you. I'm protecting you."

"Thank you for protecting me," she said sarcastically, and rolled away from him.

"Shanice..." He touched her shoulder, but she jerked away.

"Please don't touch me."

With a heavy sigh, Cruz fell back against the pillow. He watched the back of her head, desire and regret burning like acid in his gut.

After a few minutes, Shanice said, "I'm not a naïve child who needs to be coddled, Cruz. If you think I expect forever from you, I don't."

He didn't know what to say, so he said nothing.

A few more minutes passed.

"Cruz?" Shanice said timidly.

"Yes."

"I understand that nothing else can happen between us, but would you mind just holding me?"

Clearly a glutton for punishment, he put an arm around her waist and pressed his face into her fragrant dark hair. He wanted to cup her breast. He wanted to put his fingers between her legs again and touch the slick wetness that was there because of him.

"Are you punishing me now?" he asked huskily.

"No. I just want to be held."

"This might be the toughest job I've ever had. I probably won't get much sleep lying with you like this." But he'd love every minute of the torture.

She snuggled closer. "Thank you."

"You don't have to thank me for holding you. It's my pleasure."

"That's not why I'm thanking you. I'm thanking you for being honest. For being kind and not taking advantage. For everything."

"That's me, Saint Cruz."

"I'm serious," she said softly.

He closed his eyes and accepted his fate. "You're welcome, Shanice."

Eventually they drifted to sleep, with his erection pushed up against her plush buttocks.

As was his daily custom, Randall Logan sat on the back porch of his two-story Georgian house drinking his early morning black coffee. The stately mansion was his favorite and one of several he owned in the United States.

His affinity for real estate started at a young age when he used to accompany his father to collect rent payments as a child. Back then, his father had owned two duplexes and four quadruplexes, but he had never dreamed of the fortune his eldest child would eventually accrue. The truth was, his father never realized the true benefits of owning those properties.

He was too soft, always listening to the flimsy excuses from mealy-mouthed tenants about why they didn't have this month's rent or why they were late. Because of that, he was never able to expand beyond those six properties, and their family struggled financially the entire time Randall was growing up, despite having income-generating assets.

But those monthly visits taught Randall a valuable lesson. To succeed, you had to be tough. You had to be ruthless. And he had honed those traits over time and mastered them, enabling him to accumulate an enviable fortune in the real estate industry—an industry his father struggled to survive in.

Randall's son, Jacob, came through the back door onto the porch. He was dressed in a tracksuit, his black hair damp around the edges. "Good morning," he said, taking the seat beside Randall.

Randall had five children, two of them sons. Jacob was his youngest son and looked most like Randall. Perhaps that's why he had always favored him over his oldest son. Jacob had inherited his dark hair and broad forehead directly from Randall. He was also an inch over six feet, the same height as Randall, and had the build of a professional athlete because of his rigorous daily exercise regimen.

Jacob was also disciplined—another reason Randall preferred him. He never missed his workouts, and he could smell the sweat drying on his son's skin from his morning jog, a remnant of his military training.

Unfortunately, his other son, Randall Junior, was nothing like him. He was weak, like Randall's father, and couldn't stomach the gray areas Logan Investors operated in. Years ago, he left to forge his own path in the business world.

"Good morning," Randall said, eyeing his son's grave expression. "You look like you have bad news."

"It's definitely not good news. She got away."

Randall slowly set down his mug. "What about the information?"

"They weren't able to retrieve it."

Randall angled his body toward his son. "How does one woman slip away from six men sent to retrieve her and the information she's hiding?"

As soon as Randall's contact at the FBI field office discovered Shanice Lawrence was in Miami and had a copy of the information, Jacob had activated a team to pay her a visit. Ultimately, Randall wanted her dead, but not before they knew where she was hiding the data her friend Dennis had uncovered.

"She had help."

"From who?"

"Eyewitnesses say she fled the scene with a man, but I think that's impossible because all of our men were killed. One man couldn't possibly do that on his own."

"*All* of them are dead?" Randall asked, aghast.

Jacob nodded.

"What about Agent Stenson?"

"Dead."

Agent Stenson was Randall's contact at the Miami field office, a man who had started out with noble intentions, but whose gambling habit had indebted him to Randall and made him easy to control. He'd gladly gone to Shanice Lawrence's house.

"When we discovered her relationship with Dennis, we should have killed her instead of simply taking the book." Anger boiling up inside him, Randall swallowed a mouthful of coffee. The bitter taste no longer pleased him.

"That would have been unnecessary killing, and if we'd killed her, we wouldn't have known about the copy. We need to find it and any other evidence she has. Then we'll kill her."

Randall begrudgingly agreed. Maybe he was getting too impatient in his old age, but he wanted the situation with this woman tied up, fast.

"Hire people to keep an eye on the airports, bus stations, and train stations. Send them a photo of her. My guess is, she'll be on the run again, and this time harder to catch if she has help."

Jacob nodded his understanding.

"We need to find her and soon—before she and her friend figure out what those names mean."

Randall closed his fingers around the padded handle of his

cane and lifted from the chair with difficulty. His body wasn't what it used to be. He used to be active like his son, spending his leisure time running, hunting, and horseback riding. Arthritis and a car accident that badly damaged his leg made any activity difficult nowadays, but his mind was as sharp as ever, like it had been when the managers at two different properties told him about a man asking them and tenants questions. Within days, he'd discovered who Dennis Ray was and what he was up to.

If not for an overzealous police officer who had killed Dennis while trying to extract information from him, they would have wrapped up this mess a lot more smoothly.

"I need to call DC. Keep me up-to-date on the progress."

Jacob stood, too. "I will."

Randall was proud of his son and confident he would handle this problem before it got too out of control, and there was still time to do that.

He went into the house and shuffled down a long hallway to his study. With a groan, he dropped into the leather chair behind his desk and unlocked the middle drawer on the right. He picked up the phone in there and dialed the number he had memorized.

The other phone rang four times and then went to voicemail.

"I have a problem," Randall said.

Then he hung up and waited.

He expected a call back very soon.

16

Shanice awoke to the scent of cooking bacon, toast, and eggs. She'd slept soundly the night before in Cruz's arms, feeling safe for the first time in a long time.

Stretching lazily, she watched him at the kitchenette, shirtless and standing over a frying pan. Plaid boxers exposed his thick thighs and long legs dusted with curly dark hair. The sensation of one of those thighs between hers was branded into her memory. She'd welcomed the delicious tingle of hair coupled with the firmness of muscle against her skin.

Their hot and heavy make-out session had been her favorite part of sharing a bed with him. His rough hands had spiked heat in her blood and his kisses had turned her on in a way she hadn't experienced in a long time—maybe ever. She had no doubt Cruz would be an incredible lover, and the press of his hard erection against her ass had made her lady parts ache and convinced her that he could definitely satisfy her needs. But he'd been right to stop them from going any further.

Her roaming gaze paused on an old scar on his back, located a little lower and larger than the one at the front. That must be where the bullet exited. There were other marks on his skin. Fainter ones that looked like lashes, as if someone had sliced him up with a blade or the harsh, punishing end of a cat o' nine tails. The thought of anyone hurting him made her sick to her stomach. She wanted to go to him, give him a comforting hug, and kiss away the scars that marred his skin.

Shanice blinked back tears of sorrow and sat up in the bed, and Cruz twisted his head in her direction.

"Breakfast will be ready in five minutes," he said. "Did you sleep well?"

"Best sleep I've had in a long time," she admitted.

"Good." His eyes did a quick sweep of her upper body before he returned his attention to the pan.

She knew for certain that he wanted her, and though she'd been disappointed by his words last night, she appreciated that he hadn't taken advantage. Having sex with him was a bad idea. She could easily see herself falling for this man, hard, getting her emotions all tangled up in him. They didn't know what would happen in the coming days. And he'd been clear about what would happen once they figured out the relevance of the names. He would move on, and all she'd have were the memories of their time together.

She'd never see his face again. She'd never hear the low timbre of his accented voice. The thought of walking away—for good—filled her with longing. Sheesh, she was already emotionally invested and they hadn't even had sex.

Shanice went into the bathroom and washed her face and brushed her teeth. She put on her dry underwear and did her best finger-combing her hair before she examined her appearance. She wore no makeup, not even lip gloss, but this would have to do.

By the time she re-entered the main room, Cruz had placed breakfast on a couple of Styrofoam plates and poured them each a glass of orange juice in clear plastic cups.

"You're a great host," she said, aiming to keep the mood light.

"I do what I can," he joked back.

Since there was no dining table, she sat at the desk and he sat on the bed, holding his plate in his hand.

"Did you have all this food here last night, or did you leave to get us something to eat?" Shanice bit into a piece of bacon cooked to perfection. Not too crispy, exactly the way she liked.

"I left early this morning and went to the corner store to get us something to eat. I don't keep much here because I don't stay here."

"It's sort of a hideout spot?"

He smiled faintly. "You could say that."

She guessed he wouldn't tell her more and asked, "What's the plan for today?"

"We're catching a flight to Houston. Driving would be the best way to ensure we stay under the radar, but that will take too long. I have a friend who owns a Cirrus personal jet, and if I give him a little extra, he won't acknowledge that you're a passenger on the plane. Before we leave, we'll buy a burner phone, and you can call your mother and Beatrice."

"Okay."

Cruz set aside his plate on the bed. Resting his elbows on his knees, he studied her with his intense umber eyes. "Your situation could get worse before it gets better. We don't know what we'll find once we arrive in Texas. Are you up for all of this?"

Though the gravity in his voice scared her, Shanice nodded. "I want whoever murdered Dennis to be punished, and I want whatever he uncovered about them to be exposed."

"*Bueno*. Then we're on the same page."

Cruz said the pink blouse she had in her backpack didn't allow her to blend in enough, so he gave her a blue T-shirt, which she paired with skinny jeans.

He also handed her a navy-blue cap to wear and told her there was little chance of being captured on camera in a neighborhood like this—one reason the area made a good hiding place. Cameras tended to be in wealthier zip codes. Wherever there was money, there would be cameras, but he instructed her to pull the brim of the cap low on her face as an extra precaution.

"Expect the best, plan for the worst," he said.

He wore a black cap, a black T-shirt, and dark jeans. With his height and build, the outfit gave him a take-no-shit appearance that renewed her confidence she'd be safe in his care. When they were ready to go, he lifted his duffel bag onto his shoulder, and she picked up her backpack, and they left the apartment.

On the way to the store, they walked along a sidewalk littered with cigarette butts and trash, and passed a homeless man sleeping upright in the doorway of a boarded up building. A few blocks away, they entered a store with white bars over the windows and a multitude of signs offering lottery tickets, electronics, and beer within. Cruz instructed her to keep her head down, and she followed his instructions to the letter.

As he stood in line with two bottles of juice, Shanice's eyes perused the newspapers stacked at the front. Her breath suspended when she saw the headline on the front page of the *Miami Herald*: *Six Men Dead Overnight as Gunfire Erupts in Miami Suburb*.

The article mentioned the police were searching for a man and woman who'd fled the scene, and included with the article was a photo of Cruz's Mustang and two shadowy figures inside. One of the neighbors must have taken the photo with their phone.

Shanice glanced up at Cruz, whose eyes were trained on the same paper. She ducked her head again, fingers tightening on the strap of the backpack over her shoulder, worry gnawing at her insides.

The person in front of Cruz left the line and he stepped up to the counter. "I need a phone," he said, pointing at one of them hanging behind the female cashier.

He added a *Miami Herald* to his purchases and they left after he paid.

Cruz steered her to an area between two buildings. "You have five minutes," he said, handing her the phone. He then stepped away and began to read the article about them.

Shanice was curious about the contents, but she had work to do. The first person she called was Beatrice because she figured she wouldn't reach her on the cruise ship and could leave a message. She left a voicemail, apologizing for the damage to her home and letting the older woman know she was fine and would be in touch as soon as she could. She ended by thanking her for all her help and then hung up.

Then she called her mother. The conversation was much more difficult, and Shanice teared up as they talked. The fear in her mother's voice was tangible, and she hated worrying her.

"Mom, I have to go. But remember what I told you. They're coming to get you today. Get ready to leave, okay?"

"I'll be fine. I'm worried about you. Be careful. I love you," Miriam said.

"Love you, too."

After she hung up, they were on the move. Cruz separated the phone parts and dumped them into different trash bins as they walked along the sidewalk.

"What did the article say?" Shanice asked.

He handed her the paper and she scoured the contents.

"They don't have much information," Cruz summarized. "Lucky for you, you stayed under the radar at your friend's house."

"This article says that we're armed and dangerous. It makes

it sound as if you murdered those men in cold blood, but you had to kill them because they were trying to kill me."

Cruz kept up a brisk walk. "You know that, and I know that, but the police don't. All they know is that we fled the scene and left bodies behind, which looks bad."

"So we're fugitives?"

"For now. But they don't know who I am or have a clear image of who I am. They *will* figure out who you are. They're either going to think you were kidnapped, or that you were an accomplice, but we're going to clear your name, Shanice. I promise you that." The firm set of his jaw convinced her of his resolve.

Shanice folded the paper and tucked it under her arm. Outside of a speeding ticket, she'd never broken the law. Could this situation get any worse?

"I not only have to hide from the people trying to kill me, now I have to hide from the police, too."

"Another reason we need to get out of here, and fast."

They stopped at an intersection to let traffic go by. Cruz took that opportunity to dial a number on his personal phone. She listened to him make arrangements with someone—the friends he'd said owed him a favor. They would help her mother go into hiding and protect her until she and Cruz figured out what was going on with Logan Investors.

He spoke in succinct sentences, using code words like "ship the package." If she didn't know him, she wouldn't have any idea he was talking about taking her mother to safety.

They crossed the street, and after walking a few more blocks caught a taxi to a small airport thirty minutes outside of Miami. The pilot was an older Afro-Cuban, with pecan-brown skin and curious eyes when he looked at Shanice.

After the introduction, Cruz and the man stepped aside to talk and Shanice sat in the quiet terminal, watching the few passengers seated reading or talking on their phones. The airport was much quieter than Miami International Airport. Several of the passengers wore business suits. Two women looked like her and Cruz—dressed casually, flipping through magazines.

Finally, Cruz called her over, and they went onto the airfield. Shanice's steps slowed when she saw the small plane. It looked shiny and new, painted dark red along the tail and upper half and silver below.

She stopped. "That's what we're taking to Houston? You said we were going in a jet." She'd never flown in anything so small.

Cruz turned to look at her. "A *personal* jet. There's plenty of room and it's perfectly safe. Come on." He extended his hand.

Against her better judgment, Shanice placed her hand in his, and the comfort of his warm clasp lessened her anxiety.

They climbed into the surprisingly roomy interior, able to accommodate seven people comfortably in tan leather seats. Everything looked state-of-the-art, from the impressive controls on the instrument panel to the USB ports and power plugs throughout the cabin. Cruz sat next to her, smiling reassuringly and looking quite comfortable, with plenty of headroom to accommodate his height.

The pilot conducted the pre-flight check and Shanice held her breath as they taxied down the runway and lifted into the air.

Gripping the armrest to her left as she gazed out the window, her breathing slowly flattened to a normal rate, but the knots in her stomach tightened at the thought of going back to the origin of the crime. This was either a good idea or a bad idea.

She desperately hoped it was a good idea.

17

"This is home."

Cruz had checked them into a nondescript motel, someplace where they wouldn't stick out and there wasn't nosy staff providing customer service they didn't need. Almost four hours and one bag of vomit later, Shanice felt a bit tired but was in good spirits.

When they had landed, Cruz "borrowed" a gray sedan and switched the plates with a red car a mile away. Then he drove to this location on the outskirts of Houston.

He had parked far away from the front door while she hid in the back seat, out of sight. He returned with the room key and drove around to the back side where their room was located on the second floor. There wasn't much to see, but it was clean and furnished with a queen bed, a desk and chair, and a sofa beside them.

He'd tried to get a room with two beds, but the clerk told him they wouldn't have one available for two nights. Wonderful. She looked forward to two more nights of pink balls.

Shanice took a seat on the bed. "What now?" she asked.

Cruz checked his watch. "We wait."

They didn't have to wait long. A knock sounded on the door less than ten minutes later. Although he'd assured her they were safe and hadn't been followed, Cruz lifted his forefinger to his lips and signaled for her to go into the bathroom.

Heart thudding, Shanice scurried inside, turned the lock, and pressed her ear against the door. She'd be so glad when she could go back to her old comfortable life and didn't have to keep watching over her shoulder or worry every time someone came to the door.

When she heard male laughter, she knew it was safe. Raheem had arrived.

Cruz knocked on the door. "You can come out."

She exited and got her first look at Raheem, a man Cruz had spoken very little about, but each time he mentioned his name, his voice filled with admiration and affection. They were obviously very close.

Raheem was almost as tall as Cruz, with a muscular build and kind brown eyes. He had a fresh fade and a sexy grin as he extended his hand to her. She imagined he was quite a heartbreaker.

"Raheem. Nice to meet you," he said.

"Nice to meet you, too."

He looked at Cruz. "All right. Let's get down to business."

Raheem placed a silver, hard-shell suitcase on top of the desk and entered a combination. The locks flew open and revealed a laptop nestled in a black foam cushion. There were other gadgets in there, too, but he lifted out the computer and took a seat.

Cruz went to stand behind him, arms folded, brows furrowed in concentration. Shanice took a seat on the bed, where she had a good view of Raheem's screen.

"I searched for storage facilities with your friend's name," Raheem began, "but there weren't any rented in the city under Dennis Ray. I expanded my search to fifty miles outside the area, but the few I found didn't match based on the information Cruz gave me about him. I did a little more digging and found the name of his daughter and tried again. Turns out, Emily Ray is renting a unit in the Houston area, but I don't have the unit number. Give me a little time, and I can access their computer records and get everything we need."

"I would have never thought to check under his daughter's name," Shanice said, impressed.

"That's why they pay us the big bucks," Raheem said with a grin. He tapped a few keys and a window popped open on the computer. "Your friend definitely didn't want a lot of people to know he had this unit, because it's not conveniently located. The facility is thirty-two miles from here, on a low-traffic road."

"That's all wonderful, but when you find out the unit number, we won't have a key. How would we get in to see what's in the storage facility?" Shanice asked.

Cruz answered. "Let us worry about that. How much time do you need to hack their system?"

Raheem shrugged. "Less than twenty-four hours."

"We don't have that much time. I want to head over there tonight."

"I can get inside their system in minutes if I'm sitting in front of the computer."

"That's what I wanted to hear." Cruz addressed Shanice next. "Now I need you to do something. I want you to give Raheem the information, and he'll figure out what exactly these names mean. While the two of you do that, I'll order lunch."

"What kind of disk do you have?" Raheem asked.

"I don't have a disk. All the information is in my head."

He glanced at Cruz. "That's interesting."

"Before that, the names were written in a notebook," Cruz said.

Raheem nodded slowly. "Makes sense. No one can hack a notebook." He opened a new screen. "I'm ready when you are."

While Cruz ordered lunch, Shanice closed her eyes and began her recitation. There were twenty-two names in all. She also gave Raheem the dollar amounts listed next to each one. By the time she finished, Cruz was back in position behind Raheem.

Raheem hit Submit and the computer started the analysis. "This software will figure out the common denominator between all the names. Then it's going to spit out the information in a summary report to us, and we'll better understand who these people are."

The wait didn't take long at all. It couldn't have been more than a few minutes when a series of beeps alerted them of the results.

Raheem stared at the report and whistled.

"What?" Shanice leaned toward him.

"This wasn't what I expected. I thought this was some government stuff, and I guess in a way it is, but every single one of these names belongs to a police officer."

"A police officer?" Completely confused, Shanice glanced at Cruz, who wore a frown on his face.

"We're not finished. There's more." Raheem scrolled down the screen, his eyeballs swinging left to right as he digested the information. "Six of these guys have died or gone missing in the past two months. Officer Kenton and Officer Reyes never returned from a fishing trip they took. Sergeant Kelly drowned in his swimming pool. Officer Dexter and Officer Prince both had severe nut allergies and died of anaphylactic shock from accidentally eating nut-laced food. The last one, Sergeant Bing, died from carbon monoxide poisoning. There was an undetected leak in her furnace."

Not one of them said a word for at least a full minute.

"Were there any dates on the list Dennis gave you?" Cruz asked Shanice.

She shook her head. "I gave Raheem everything I know. That's all the information that I received from Dennis in the notebook."

Placing his hands on the armrests, Raheem leaned back in the chair. "This guy, Logan, probably? He buys cops. We don't know why he buys them, but he does. That has to be what the money means, right? But whenever he's done, he just kills them?"

"Wouldn't someone notice a bunch of cops suspiciously dying over such a short period?" Shanice asked.

"If they were in the same precinct, maybe. But all of these officers are spread out across five states. Only two of them were in the same precinct, and that was Officer Kenton and Officer Reyes."

"More than ever, we need to get inside that storage unit," Cruz said. "That's where the answers lie."

"What the hell had Dennis uncovered?" Shanice had said the words quietly to herself, but Cruz heard.

"Whatever it is, it was worth killing for," he said.

SHANICE WOKE up in time to see Cruz stepping out of the bathroom. He was dressed in all black—clothes he'd picked up over an hour ago when he left the room to get snacks and new clothes for both of them to wear. She'd decided to take a nap, which had lasted much longer than she'd expected. Outside was dark, and Cruz had turned on a lamp with a low wattage bulb that barely illuminated the room. Soon he and Raheem would be leaving to go to the storage facility.

Cruz had made the decision to leave her there while they were gone because he thought it was safer. She thought she would be safer, too, but was still a nervous ball of energy as she watched him get ready to leave.

She sat up in the bed and ran her fingers through her hair.

"No one knows you're here, but..." He showed her a small handgun in the palm of his hand. "Have you ever used one of these?"

"A long time ago, my father took me to the firing range. But I don't like guns."

"You don't have to like it, but it could save your life. I'm going to give you a quick refresher."

She scooted to the edge of the bed, and he spent the next few minutes showing her how to disengage the safety when she was ready to pull the trigger. He gave her advice on how to shoot, reminding her to fire at center mass.

"Got it?" he asked.

"Got it."

"If for some reason Raheem and I don't come back—"

"Don't say that!" Panic filled her.

His features softened. "Remember, I always expect the best but plan for the worst. If for some reason we don't come back, call this number." He handed her a piece of paper torn from the pad on the desk. He'd written a name and number with a DC area code below it.

Miles.

"He'll know what to do. He'll be able to help you. You already know how to stay off the grid. All you have to do is be careful. Be paranoid. Use your fear and let that guide your actions."

She nodded. "A healthy dose of fear is a good thing."

"That's right. Anyone come through that door, blow a hole in his chest."

He made it sound so easy, but shooting someone wasn't that simple. Even in situations of extreme fear, people sometimes couldn't pull the trigger. Cruz clearly didn't suffer from such hesitations.

"Got it."

A knock sounded on the door.

"That's Raheem. Time to go. I'll see you later." He headed to the door.

"Wait!"

She rushed over. Impulsively, she stood on tiptoe and gave him a quick kiss. Their lips seared together, and for a brief moment, warmth filled her belly, chasing away the ball of anxiety lodged in her chest.

"Please be careful," she whispered, gazing into his eyes.

"Always."

He cradled the back of her head with one hand and kissed her warmly and thoroughly. Tightening her fingers on his broad shoulders, she pressed into him and reveled in the pressure of his mouth against hers.

The kiss stoked the flames of her hunger for him. She wanted him, needed him so badly, and wished she were bold enough to articulate that need.

When he released her lips, his dark eyes were darker. Her heart thundered in her chest and the area at the apex of her thighs dampened with raw need. She'd never experienced such a vortex of emotion for any man.

Cruz locked eyes with her, that inscrutable expression he liked to wear firmly planted on his face. For a split second she thought he was about to say something, but his lips firmed.

And then he was gone.

18

Cruz and Raheem watched the storage facility from an empty lot across the street. They'd been there over an hour, observing the activity in and out of the fenced property.

The businesses on either side were already closed this time of night, and at the back of the facility there were warehouses —also closed with no visible activity within.

They had two minor problems to circumvent. To get onto the property, customers had to pull up to the gate and punch in a code to make the gate slide open. The other issue was the camera over the front door, which led into the office they needed to break into.

A white SUV pulled out of the lot and drove away. Based on what they'd seen before, there wouldn't be another vehicle for at least ten minutes.

"You ready?" Cruz asked.

"Born ready," Raheem answered. He pulled a skullcap low on his head and picked up a brown bag made of worn, cracked leather from the floor.

Both dressed in black, they exited the vehicle and waited on the sidewalk until a car passed before they ran across the street and jogged along the chain-link fence that enclosed the lot. Once they were in a dark area with limited visibility from the street, Cruz pulled himself up the fence while Raheem kept an eye out. Cruz landed lightly on the other side, and then Raheem climbed over while he stood watch. They took off for the front, staying in the shadows and hugging the long building which held multiple units.

At the end, Cruz peered around the corner, and headlights swept the front as a yellow car turned toward the gate. He pulled back out of sight, pressing flush against the brick. They'd wanted to be inside the office before the next car arrived. They listened to the gate scrape open on rusty wheels, and then the vehicle drove in. As luck would have it, the driver went down another row.

"We don't know how long they'll be here. I say we go in," Cruz whispered. He would have preferred that there be no one in the yard, but that renter could be back there for a long time. Better to take their chances to get the information they needed.

With a curt nod, Raheem confirmed that he agreed.

Cruz peered around the corner again to make sure they didn't have more visitors. The street out front was empty. He pulled a miniature can of black spray paint from the front pocket of his jeans. The container was small, only about three inches long with the circumference of a tube of lipstick. It was used as touch-up paint but would serve another purpose tonight.

The camera was angled toward the front door, which meant he was in its blind spot coming from the opposite direction. He stood out of sight underneath and, careful to keep his hand out of view, sprayed the paint upward over the lens, blacking out its line of sight.

Dropping to his haunches, he pulled two simple tools from the lock pick set in his back pocket and opened the door. He'd already jammed the frequency for the alarm system while they were across the street, so now they had no additional barriers to entry.

With a low whistle, he signaled to Raheem that the door was open, and they both slipped inside. The office was small and dark, but light came in through the window from a light post on the street. Staying in the shadows against the wall, Cruz kept an eye on the outdoors. They didn't anticipate anyone from the company showing up because no one watched the camera's live feed. A small outfit like this would rely on recording the security footage. They likely wouldn't notice anything was wrong with the camera outside unless they paid close attention to it or someone had a reason to review the recorded footage.

Raheem went behind the counter and connected an electronic box to the computer. A red light came on. Cruz had no idea what that device was called, but what he did know was that it would help Raheem hack into the system.

"What's the deal with Shanice?" his friend asked.

"What do you mean?" Cruz kept his eyes focused on the street outside.

"She's a looker. I'm wondering if she's single."

That drew his attention. It was no secret how much Raheem enjoyed women. He was a veritable ladies' man. "Why?"

His friend glanced up at him. "Thinking about taking a chance on her since you don't seem to want to mix business with pleasure this time. I don't put those kinds of limitations on myself."

That much was true. Raheem had left a string of broken hearts around the world.

"You're a regular Romeo," Cruz said dryly.

He'd had a hard time walking away from Shanice tonight and wasn't used to the type of conversation they'd had before he left the motel. He and the men and women he sometimes worked with cared about each other, but only as it related to the completion of a mission. They had to work together and cover each other's back.

What she had expressed back there was...different. Genuine concern that had little to do with his ability to help her fully understand what happened to Dennis and why. She had been concerned about *Cruz*—as a person—and that was a different sentiment altogether. His chest tightened as he reflected on her words. *Please be careful.*

"Do you mind if I make a move on her?" Raheem asked.

"Yes, I do." Cruz returned his attention to outside the window.

"Why would you mind?"

Irritation billowed up inside him. "Mind your fucking business and finish the job," Cruz snapped.

Raheem laughed softly. He'd recognized Cruz's feelings for Shanice and baited him, and Cruz had fallen for the bait.

"We're in."

The red light had turned green and Raheem disconnected the machine from the computer. "Dennis Ray,' he mumbled to himself as he typed.

At the sound of a car's engine, Cruz returned his attention to the window. He eased out of the line of sight and watched the yellow car leave. Without having to be told, Raheem had ducked behind the counter.

When the gate was closed, Cruz said, "They're gone."

Raheem stood and quickly tapped his fingers across the keyboard. "Got it. Unit 1120. That all we need?"

"That's it."

Raheem logged off the computer and they left, locking the door on the way out. They went down a far row until they came to 1120. Cruz picked the lock and yanked the rolling door upward.

They slipped in and rolled the door back down.

Raheem turned on his flashlight, and they stared at the only item in the tiny unit—a cardboard bankers box.

"This is it?" Raheem asked.

Cruz walked across the dusty cement floor to the box and crouched down. "He wasn't storing any personal belongings here, which means he'd gotten this facility for the sole purpose of hiding his research." He removed the lid.

Shining the light inside, they picked out notebooks and files stuffed full of papers and photos.

They took their time combing through them. The first two folders didn't have anything to do with Logan Investors, but when Raheem turned several pages of the third folder, he said with a burst of excitement in his voice, "Check this out."

Cruz set aside the documents he'd been perusing and took a look. He couldn't believe what he saw. There was lots of information showing Dennis's research on Logan Investors, including a background on the company, a list of their holdings across the country, and pages and pages of notes.

Not only that, there were photos, which looked like they had been taken from a distance. One man showed up in several of the photos and looked so much like Randall, Cruz had to assume that he was his son. But the most interesting photo was near the back of the stack. That contained a shot of Randall and Senator Sandoval holding rifles, as if they were on a hunting trip. There was a cluster of trees and a cabin in the back. Both men had their arms around each other and were grinning widely into the camera's lens. They looked younger and more vibrant than their current age of men in their sixties. He guessed them to be in their late thirties or early forties in the shot.

"Wait a minute, does this mean what I think it means? Is the senator involved with Logan Investors?" Raheem said.

Cruz rubbed his jaw. "Maybe, but my question is, if he is— what exactly are they involved in? And did his niece know?"

"She probably didn't know about the information her husband had collected on Logan."

"Which means she wouldn't know her uncle was implicated." Cruz shook his head. "Their friendship obviously goes back a couple of decades."

"One or both of them had a team go after Shanice. If you hadn't been nearby..."

Cruz's chest burned when he considered what those men would have done to her to get the information. If she didn't talk, they would have tortured her the same way they did Dennis.

"We're taking the whole box and sorting through the contents tonight." Cruz replaced the lid.

"Think about the scandal if this gets out. Logan Investors is bribing and killing cops, and that's only part of this puzzle. They're covering something up. Why are they bribing them? If the senator is involved in this..." Raheem looked at Cruz.

Cruz finished the sentence. "He'll do anything to keep it quiet."

19

T he box Raheem and Cruz had taken from the storage facility sat on the floor, but the contents were spread out on the desk like dinner plates.

They had removed everything related to Logan Investors and the investigation Dennis had launched against the company. All three of them scoured the files for details. Raheem sat at the desk, Shanice on the bed, and Cruz on the sofa, his long legs propped on the mattress beside her, feet crossed at the ankles.

"I'm more convinced than ever that Dennis didn't kill himself," Shanice said.

Cruz was convinced, too. He shifted through the sheets, studying all the clues her friend had left behind. The name Precise, LLC was circled on a piece of paper, and the rest of Dennis's handwritten notes conveyed an alarming pattern. Whenever Logan couldn't get control of a property in an up-and-coming neighborhood, he "worked" with the local police department, which increased police presence in the neighborhoods by ticketing and towing cars, arresting people for jaywalking, and conducting raids on the tenants—many of whom were on government assistance—after getting anonymous "tips."

Raheem shook his head. "During those raids, they always found drugs, which is a violation of the lease agreements and gets the tenants kicked off government assistance."

"Mass evictions, and then within months Logan buys the cash-strapped property and moves forward," Shanice finished.

"Forced gentrification by cop," Raheem said bitterly.

"Most of these tenants were older, disabled, or single moms," Shanice said, her voice filled with horror as she reviewed the papers in her hands.

Anger burned through Cruz as he thought about what those people went through. "Not only did Dennis find a pattern connecting the raids to Logan's properties, but there's clearly some kind of relationship—or at least he suspected there was a relationship—between Logan and Senator Sandoval."

"Just because Logan knew the senator doesn't mean that he was involved," Shanice countered.

Cruz closed the folder he was reviewing and set it on the cushion beside him. "The fact that Dennis had a photo of the two of them makes me think that's what he suspected. And frankly, it's very uncommon for there to be such a huge coincidence." Rubbing the back of his neck, he let everything he knew turn around in his head.

"Do you think Karen Sandoval is involved?" Raheem asked.

"I believe she told the truth as she knew it. I don't think she knew about her uncle, and if Dennis was smart, he didn't mention what he found out to her. He knew he'd have to get proof. Without that, he'd jeopardize a reconciliation with his wife for no reason."

"He said nothing and kept digging," Raheem posited.

Cruz nodded. "They eventually found out what he knew, or maybe he went to Logan and threatened him. Who knows what he did, but somehow they found out what he was doing and had him arrested."

"Planting drugs on him was easy since it's what they often do in these raids," Shanice said.

"Let's think about what we have here," Cruz said. "We have bribery, that's no doubt. What we don't have is a direct link showing Logan Investors actually paid these officers to conduct the raids. We have circumstantial evidence, and a good attorney could get this information dismissed, no matter how damaging we think it is. We need concrete proof that he paid these officers. We also need concrete proof that Senator Sandoval is involved."

"How do we prove any of that? Dennis didn't seem capable of putting together proof, even though he had connected the dots." Raheem set aside his file.

"We'll have to go to the source," Cruz said.

"Logan?" Raheem asked.

"Yes."

"Tell me you have a plan."

Cruz smiled crookedly. "I do. We need to get into Logan Towers."

Raheem's eyes lit up. "You're thinking about doing a computer dump."

"Exactly. But not his computer. Guys like Randall Logan don't do their own dirty work, and whatever he does, he'll want it to look legit, which means he's probably got a company set up that will take care of the payments, which will look like regular old business expenses. We need to go to accounting."

"I have the perfect program to take care of the dump," Raheem said.

Cruz stretched an arm along the back of the sofa. "And I know how we'll get inside the accounting office. We set off the fire alarm, then you and I go in and dump the computer files onto your external drive."

He laid out the plan, with Raheem nodding his agreement at various points. When he finished, there was silence as both men turned the idea around in their heads, checking for flaws.

"I could help," Shanice piped up from the bed.

They both looked at her.

"No," Cruz said.

She looked crushed. "Why not?"

"Because I said so."

She opened her mouth to protest, but Raheem interjected, "Actually, her suggestion kind of makes sense. If she goes in ahead of us and hits the alarm, she could leave with the crowd and disappear, then you and I could go up."

"*No.* We stick to the plan I laid out. You set off the alarm, and I'll come in as backup."

"Cruz—"

"I said no, and that's final. I won't risk her getting hurt. We're the professionals. If something goes wrong..." He stopped talking because his voice had thickened with worry.

"I feel like a burden. Let me help," Shanice implored.

"You're not a burden, and we can find something else for you to do."

"Like what, Cruz? Sit here and wait until you come back? I *want* to do this, and based on the plan you laid out, having me help will make your life easier. If you have a third person set off the alarm, you can both be in disguise without having to change in the building, and then you'll have less chance of getting caught. Let me help, please. Dennis was my friend, and I want these bastards to pay for what they did to him and for what they're doing to these tenants. Let me do *something.*"

Raheem averted his eyes and became preoccupied with one of the open files on the desk.

Cruz dropped his feet to the floor and sighed heavily. Her impassioned, pleading voice was his undoing. When he spoke, his voice was heavy with the gravity of what they were about to do. "You get in and get out. You understand me?"

Her eyes lit up, and she nodded, but he didn't like the idea of her going to Logan Investors one bit.

With reservations, Cruz said, "Okay, here's the plan…"

FROM THE DOORWAY of the bathroom, Cruz watched Shanice. He'd hoped she would already be in bed. The room was small but seemed smaller with her standing half naked in the low light cast by the lamp on the nightstand. If he stretched out a hand, he could touch her soft skin and lose himself in her sweet embrace like he had earlier when they hugged goodbye.

His loins still ached from that brief contact, and watching her bent over the sofa, digging around inside her backpack, didn't help. The curved underside of her backside peeked from beneath the hem of the shirt and made blood rush to his groin.

He'd almost followed Raheem out the door to avoid spending another night alone with her. He wanted her too much, and this close proximity didn't help. He kept imagining her naked and reliving the night before when he'd fingered her. The only thing saving him from going crazy was his ability to compartmentalize, but he was having a hell of a time doing so.

Cruz rubbed the back of his neck, wondering if he'd made a mistake by including her in tomorrow's little project to break into the accounting office at Logan Investors. He knew the dangers involved in the work they did. If someone recognized her or anything at all went wrong, they could grab her and hurt her to get the information they wanted.

"You're very brave," he said.

She turned at the sound of his voice. "Not brave. I want to help, like I said. Doesn't mean I'm not scared."

He walked over to where she stood. Looking deeply into her

eyes, he said, "It's okay if you change your mind. I won't get mad, and I won't judge you. Neither will Raheem."

"I won't change my mind."

She spoke with such confidence that she actually put his mind at ease a little bit. Maybe she could handle this. Maybe she wasn't as fragile as he thought, but that didn't mean he wasn't worried about her welfare.

"Just remember the plan. If anything goes wrong, you call us and we'll be right there. Got it? They won't get you out of that building without going through me first."

She smiled. "Stop worrying."

"I can't help but worry," he said gruffly, walking by her. He stuck the last folder in the box on the desk and placed the lid on top.

"I trust you. I trust the plan. I'm not worried because I've seen how you work, and I know we'll get through this just fine."

"You're that confident in me?"

"Yes. I know that confiding in you was the right decision," she said in a soft voice.

Her eyes drifted over his bare chest, and desire filtered into her eyes. His traitorous manhood swelled in response.

His reason for coming into her life might have been fake, but this constant hunger he felt and saw reciprocated in her eyes—that wasn't fake. He figured she found him attractive because he was different and not like the men she was used to. Maybe there was a little hero worship involved, but she shouldn't want a man like him. Within her was innocence and light, but he'd seen the ugliest of humanity. He wasn't innocent, and his world was filled with darkness.

"Don't look at me like that," he said, sounding like he had a tennis ball lodged in his throat.

"I can't help it."

She cast her eyes downward, and he let out a raspy laugh filled with longing and swiped a hand down his face.

Nothing should happen between them. That's what he told her, right? A little more than twenty-four hours ago, and he was already contemplating going back on his word.

She's turned me into a liar, he thought with disgust. A horny, pathetic liar with a dick so hard he needed relief.

He took a single step toward her, and her head tipped back to look up at him. "I don't want to hurt you, Shanice. Do you understand that?"

"Yes."

Cruz cursed softly, eyes laser-focused on the fullness of her mouth.

She wasn't like the other women he encountered during his line of work. She wasn't a hardened criminal determined to hurt the government or its citizens. She wasn't a fellow assassin who wore an invisible cloak of steel to protect against falling prey to feelings and emotional entanglements that could jeopardize a mission. Shanice was a civilian and could become attached, which meant he could seriously hurt her when he left her behind.

Which is why what he planned to do made him the worst kind of selfish prick. Telling himself she was an adult and knew what she wanted didn't help.

He threaded his fingers into her soft hair and tilted back her head. Her eyes fluttered closed and her chest heaved as the rate of her breathing increased.

He knew better. He should stop. But he didn't.

20

C ruz kissed her, his mouth moving over her soft lips with urgency. He wanted to kiss her all the time and couldn't remember another woman whose mouth he'd ever enjoyed as much.

Warmth seeped into his limbs as she pressed her body against his. His hands slid down her sides and then moved back up her rib cage to close over her breasts. She moaned into his mouth, and he drizzled kisses along the arch of her neck. Sucking gently on her collarbone, he moved her backward toward the bed.

They lowered onto the firm mattress and he pressed between her welcoming thighs. Impatiently, he ground his hips into hers while taking his time to kiss her properly. Her mouth was succulent and sweet, and the scent of her skin was intoxicating and provocative.

He wanted her, *needed* her so badly and struggled to control his intense reaction to having her in his arms, worried he'd frighten her with the driving need to conquer and devour. He sucked on her bottom lip and grated her chin with his teeth. Holding her head steady with one hand, his tongue sought refuge in her mouth, claiming her as his with deep, leisurely strokes.

He couldn't get enough and groaned when she arched into him, whispering his name and raking her fingers through his hair. Using her whimpering mewls as a guide, Cruz removed her shirt and continued to explore her body. His tongue flicked across the tips of her breasts, and the caramel nipples grew hard beneath the ministrations of his mouth. He squeezed their softness and sucked with the abandon of a newborn, giving each breast the attention it so richly deserved.

While he dragged his tongue along the curved underside of one breast, he let his fingers move over the curve of her hips and between her thighs. He rubbed her sex, using her body's moisture to glide a finger over the turgid clit hidden between the wet folds.

Grasping one leg, he drew her thighs apart and placed a soft kiss at the side of her knee. His lips skimmed lower, slowly savoring each newly explored inch of silky golden skin. He could smell her arousal, and the scent tempted him to edge closer and closer to his target.

She whimpered when he reached the crease that connected her thigh to her pelvis.

"Cruz, I—"

"Shh. Let me..."

He flicked his tongue against her clit, sampling the delicious honey between her legs. On a ragged moan, she pleaded with him to stop and fuck her, but he knew she didn't mean it. Her thighs had fallen open wider, and she strained up into his mouth, clamping one hand at the back of his head. Those were the actions of a woman in the throes of passion. A woman who didn't want him to stop.

He buried his face in heaven, sucking on her engorged clitoris and licking at the moisture that professed her hunger for him. He feasted on her slick lips, ruthlessly getting her off with his tongue while depriving her of his dick.

When she came, her breathy moans turned into hoarse cries of satisfaction. Twisting and turning, she trembled through her climax, and only when he lifted his mouth from her flesh did she finally relax.

Cruz wiped his mouth clean and then kissed his way back up her body. She was panting now, begging even more for him to take her. "Please, *please*," she whispered.

He smiled to himself, her enthusiasm its own special aphrodisiac. And who was he to deny her? He was certain he could not deny this woman anything she asked for.

Cruz got a condom and then removed his boxers. She was so goddamn eager for the dick, he barely had time to haul off her panties before she was pulling him on top of her.

He slipped in, merging their bodies and moaning into her neck. The tight, wet fit felt so damn good. He knew right away he wanted more of her. More of this. Too much would not be enough. When this investigation was over, he didn't know what would become of them, but for now he would enjoy every minute in her presence and every second between her thighs.

His thrusts increased in tempo as his climax neared. A bead of sweat trickled down his spine as pressure built in his balls. He felt the moment an orgasm rippled through her and the tightening of her internal muscles around his length.

Fingers gripping the sheets, he thrust harder. Grunting, he lifted his head to stare down into her face. What a sight to behold, this thick, beautiful, sexy woman lost in the mind-numbing throes of ecstasy. Eyes closed, cheeks flushed, her open lips letting loose hoarse cries of passion.

Cruz lifted her leg just below the knee and angled his body to go deeper. The volume of her rapturous cries increased, making goose bumps rise on his skin.

He would have to remember this exact position to bring her

to climax again, but for now all he could do was give in to the relentless undulating motion of her hips and the aggressive orgasm that throbbed impatiently in his groin.

Cum shot out of his body, and he was certain nothing had ever felt this good. Not even the successful completion of a mission, which used to be the ultimate high.

He cursed repeatedly in Spanish until his tense, quaking body finally collapsed from the excruciating pleasure. He fell on top of her, depleted of his strength and ability to move.

DID anything feel as good as the warm, postcoital embrace of a man's arms?

Cruz smoothed a hand up and down Shanice's back, and she moaned, stretching and rubbing against his hard body. She'd for sure sleep well tonight, but she didn't feel like sleeping right now. She wanted to remain awake so she could continue to enjoy snuggling with him in the dark. When morning came, their mission to get inside the Logan Investors office would interrupt this comfy feeling like sunlight interrupts the darkness of night.

"What was your life like growing up?" Cruz asked.

Shanice considered the question before answering honestly. "Fun, for the most part. My parents were very strict and I led a sheltered life. I didn't get to go to a lot of parties and do the normal things kids and teenagers do where they stay out late and get into trouble. Most of the time I was at home with my mother and father. When I was old enough to go out on the weekends, I was always with my cousins. I still had fun, but for other people it might be considered boring."

He played with a curl near her ear. "You were a good girl."

She laughed. "Pretty much. I never got into trouble, and I

obeyed curfew, the whole bit. A complete and total goody two-shoes."

"There's nothing wrong with that," Cruz said. "I could've used some restraint when I was younger."

She shifted her head on the pillow to get a good look at him. "Tell me something about yourself."

He looked at her and she waited, hoping he would share. Cruz was guarded and had erected barriers between them, but she wanted to know him, really know him. Not the persona he originally presented but the man—the real man beneath the code of silence and abs of steel.

"Living in Cuba, I often felt like my life was destined for a dead-end," he said, starting slowly, as if trying out this idea of sharing a part of himself. "My parents died when I was young, and I didn't have any brothers and sisters. My father's mother lived in Canada, so I went to live with my mother's mother when I was nine. Like a lot of the older folks, she was satisfied with her life, but I was like many of the young people. We were restless and wanted something more. We wanted more freedom, and for us, the United States was where we wanted to be. The first time I tried to come here, we were stopped by the Coast Guard and turned around."

"That must've been difficult," Shanice said.

"Very. We had drifted on the water for twenty-five days, so to have to go back was very disappointing. That didn't stop us though. We made our second attempt six months later and were successful. I was fifteen. I stayed with an uncle and aunt who had immigrated to the States many years before. I went back a handful of times to see my maternal grandmother, before she died."

"How did you end up working for the government? You never really explained to me who you work for, either. Are you CIA?" She hoped her many questions didn't cause him to clam up.

"I don't work for the CIA or FBI." He paused. "I work for an agency that officially doesn't exist. Unofficially, we're part of the U.S. Department of Justice. Our job is to protect the country from domestic and international threats. The agency is always on the lookout for new recruits, usually people like me—troublemakers, preferably with no close family ties. If you're a smart criminal, even better. They can use your criminal background as leverage to convince you to work for them. I was constantly in trouble, and they approached me when I was in jail for beating the crap out of a guy who assaulted a girl in the bathroom of a house party I'd attended. It wasn't my first assault charge. Since I was eighteen and faced a long stretch, working for them was an appealing alternative."

"If your agency doesn't exist, what happens if you're hurt or...die?" Her voice shook on the last word.

He shrugged. "Nothing. The government would act as if they never heard of me, and they'll behave as if they didn't send me on the mission."

"But if you work for the Department of Justice—"

"We work for the department, but we're not restricted by their guidelines and protocols."

"Oh." Shanice played with a hair on his chest. "If you weren't doing this kind of work, what would you be doing?"

"You're full of questions tonight, aren't you?"

"Do you mind? I just want to know a little bit about the man I slept with."

"Fair enough," he said with a healthy dose of humor in his voice. "Assuming I stayed out of trouble, I'd probably start my own security firm. I like what I do, but I sometimes think about having a normal eight-to-five job—or as normal as security could be."

"You should do what makes you happy. I hope you get a chance to do that one day, although it still sounds dangerous."

"Not as dangerous as what I do now, trust me. And thank you, I hope I do get to open my own firm one day, too."

She kissed his shoulder and took a big whiff of his skin. Leather and citrus. "Thank you for sharing with me."

He held her tighter, running his rough hands over her back and sliding his fingers up into her curly hair. "You're easy to talk to."

She purred as his fingers massaged her scalp. "One more question, and I promise that's it."

He chuckled softly and let his hand rest on the middle of her back. "Go ahead."

"I know you're good at what you do, but do you ever get worried that you might mess up? Like back at Beatrice's house, when you told me to duck. What if you'd missed?"

"Missed?" he repeated, as if that was a foreign word.

"Yes, miss. People miss, Cruz. What if you'd missed him, or worse—hit me."

"No way. In a situation like that, I'm too focused. I never miss."

"You've never ever missed?"

"Never, *mami*. Not once. You doubt me?" Amusement seeped back into his eyes.

"Noooo. Who would dare doubt the mighty Cruz?"

"Sounds like you're being sarcastic, and I don't like it. But for the record, only a fool would doubt me."

"All right." She sighed but smiled softly. "When do we go to Logan Towers tomorrow?"

"Raheem and I want to check out the building, and he's going to pull up the floor plan. You're coming with us because you'll need to pick up a disguise, and we'll need to get supplies. We'll head over to Logan Towers near the end of the day when people are less alert and ready to go home."

"I'll be ready."

"You're one hundred percent certain you want to do this?" Cruz asked.

"One thousand percent," she said with confidence.

"What am I going to do with you?" He gave her a crooked smile and leaned in for a kiss.

Shanice eagerly kissed him back. The searing tongue kiss consumed her with its heat and made desire pool anew between her thighs.

When he pushed her onto her back, she shoved her fingers into his soft hair, spread her legs, and pulled him close—anxious for him to take possession of her body once again.

21

Shanice walked into the Logan Towers building as if she belonged there, but she carried a swarm of butterflies in her stomach.

Cruz had wanted her to blend in with the people coming and going from the building, so she was dressed in a gunmetal-gray pantsuit, heels, and wore a brunette wig cut in a short bob. She also wore non-prescription glasses as part of her disguise.

Besides the one security guard, there were only a few people in the lobby, and he wasn't paying attention to anyone because his eyes were focused on an iPad in his hand. Logan's office was on the top floor, but his accounting department was three floors below, on the eleventh. The plan was for her to go to that floor and set up the diversion.

She walked into the elevator with two men. The younger one didn't pay her any attention, too busy arguing with someone on his Bluetooth. The other person, an older gentleman, smiled and she returned the friendly greeting, hoping he didn't notice how nervous she was.

The three of them rode up in silence, but the men exited on lower floors. Shanice breathed easier as she continued to her destination, careful to keep her head turned away from the camera in the corner, preventing them from getting a good image of her profile, just in case.

When she walked off the elevator, she moved slowly down the hall, eyes searching for the ladies' restroom. According to the floor plan Raheem had pulled up, it should be right...*there* —almost at the end, situated between two closed office doors.

Shanice slipped in and checked under each stall door to make sure she was alone. Then she went into the one at the far end and locked the door. Her pulse was racing, and she took a moment to calm down, briefly closing her eyes. Before coming here she'd been pretty confident, but now that she had to carry out her part of the plan, nerves were eating her alive.

"You've got to do this. Cruz and Raheem are depending on you. Do it for Dennis."

The pep talk was enough to prompt her into removing the contents in her mostly empty shoulder bag. The plan was for her to create an explosion that caused the entire building to be evacuated. Cruz had shown her how to make the makeshift bomb, and they'd had a practice run in an empty parking lot earlier. She could definitely do this, she just needed to stop shaking.

After giving herself another stern talking to, Shanice took out a napkin and a water bottle half-filled with white vinegar. Cruz had rolled up the napkin like a blunt with baking soda inside. She was about to drop it into the bottle when the bathroom door creaked open.

She stopped.

As footsteps clicked across the tile floor and ended in the stall next door, she listened intently, belly bunched into knots. There was no way the other person could possibly know what she was doing, but her heart hammered nonetheless.

The other bathroom occupant flushed the commode and then her heels snapped across the tile again. She washed her hands and then exited, and Shanice relaxed and resumed the task at hand.

She dropped the baking soda-filled napkin into the bottle and quickly screwed on the cap as the liquid fizzed and expanded inside the plastic container. She left the stall, and with a brisk walk opened the bathroom door and peered into the hall. Empty. Now for the diversion part.

Shanice lifted the bottle, flung it with all her might toward the far wall, and dashed away. A loud boom pushed through the slowly closing door and echoed in the hallway.

Shanice clutched her chest, caught off guard by the volume of the noise. The explosion was louder than the practice one she'd detonated earlier. This sounded like a real bomb.

Hurrying down the hallway, she pulled the fire alarm and resumed her brisk walk. A few people rushed out of their offices, eyes wide and questioning.

"What was that?" an older man yelled over the ringing.

"I don't know," Shanice answered. "Sounded like an explosion and then the fire alarm went off."

"I thought I heard an explosion, too."

"I'm getting out of here." She hurried to the emergency exit and pushed into the stairwell. Since the fire alarm had been pulled, the elevators in the building became inoperable, forcing everyone to take the stairs.

Shanice hurried downward, the sound of others rushing behind her. People crowded into the stairwell from the lower and upper floors, and they all made a haphazard, unorganized descent toward the ground.

She had to refrain from smiling. She'd done it!

The next step was up to Cruz and Raheem.

∾

SEATED in the stolen gray car between two buildings, Cruz and Raheem watched from across the street as people poured from Logan Towers. Cruz had set the timer on his watch the minute the fire alarm went off. He could already hear the fire truck sirens and glanced at his watch.

"They're ahead of time," he remarked.

"Even better," Raheem said from the passenger seat.

Less than a minute later, the fire truck parked in the middle of the street, and firefighters started to disembark.

"We're up," Cruz said.

He and Raheem were dressed like firefighters, including the helmets. As the men and women darted from the building, they pushed against the rushing tide to enter. Cruz caught sight of Shanice and their gazes locked momentarily. Relief flooded him, knowing she was getting out without a hitch. He also experienced an overwhelming sense of pride. He was proud of her, and he'd let her know that later.

He and Raheem raced up the stairs, all the way to the eleventh floor. They stepped into the hall and into silence and went straight to the accounting office. Cruz turned the handle and the door swung open.

The huge room contained eight desks, all with computers and papers stacked on top of them. There was a smaller office to the left with a frosted glass door.

"Accounting manager's office," Raheem said, heading over there. The door was locked.

Without prompting, he slammed his heel next to the knob. The frame splintered and the door swung open, crashing against the inside wall. He pulled his tools from under the bulky firefighter's coat and dropped into the manager's chair. He connected a machine to the computer and started downloading the files.

"How long?" Cruz asked, checking his watch.

"He or she has quite a bit on here, so about seven minutes."

Cruz ambled over to the window. A swarm of people stood around in the street and on the sidewalks. Workers from the other buildings were also coming out to stare and find out what was going on. Before too long, they would discover there wasn't a fire.

They had decided to have Shanice place the "bomb" on the eleventh floor because it would take longer for the firefighters to get up to that floor and figure out that something was wrong. Also because there were fewer suites on that floor, which meant fewer people.

"Hey, what are you doing in here?" The voice came from the doorway.

Cruz snapped around.

Shit.

He hadn't expected anyone to be up there. He put a disarming smile on his face and approached the two security guards, quickly sizing them up.

The big brunette might be a problem, but the smaller Black man held a walkie-talkie and looked unsure that he wanted to interrupt. His expression suggested he didn't get paid enough to deal with what was coming his way.

"Checking out the office to make sure everything is okay in here." Cruz stood in the doorway, blocking Raheem from view.

"Doesn't look like that's what you're doing to me. Why's he on that computer?" The brunette angled his body to the side in an effort to look around him.

"He had to check something real quick," Cruz said.

He landed three quick jabs to the man's solar plexus and caught him off guard. He doubled over and Cruz flung a kick at the stunned Black man's head. He crashed into a desk and passed out on the floor.

Cruz was about to pick up the walkie-talkie, but was grabbed from behind in a bear hug. More irritated than worried, he propelled himself backward and slammed them into the wall. The brunette groaned when his spine hit, and Cruz followed up by jerking his arms upward, loosening the other man's grip. He sidestepped and brought him over his shoulder, tossing him hard to the floor.

The man groaned again, and Cruz yanked him up by the collar and thrust him headfirst into the wall, knocking him unconscious. He fell backward and dropped to the carpet, arms spread-eagle.

"Wrong day to try to be a hero." Cruz tossed the walkie-talkie aside and took the Black guard's handcuff and latched him to the foot of a desk. He took the other man's handcuff and secured him to the Black guard. Then he removed their keys and phones and chucked them across the room.

"Almost done," Raheem called.

Cruz re-entered the office. "You could have helped me."

"I knew you had it." His friend grinned. What seemed like almost no time later, he said, "Done," and jumped up from the chair.

The two of them exited the office and started down the stairs. Two firemen were on their way up.

"Did you see anything?" the one in front asked.

"*Nada*," Cruz answered, and continued walking. He and Raheem exited the building and went back to the alley where they had kept watch.

Raheem removed his laptop from the trunk and they tossed in the uniforms.

They took off in the car, Cruz driving.

"Let's see what we have," Raheem said from the backseat, and turned on the computer.

22

Shanice sat with tense shoulders on a stool in Starbucks, staring out the window, fingers clasped around an empty cup. This was the rendezvous point, and as soon as Cruz and Raheem were finished, they'd come to pick her up.

To her right was a man typing away on his laptop, and on her left was a woman whispering into a phone. Neither one of them paid attention to her, but she was very aware of her surroundings and closely watched each person who entered and exited through the door.

She had no idea what she was looking for. A tic. An odd glance in her direction. Anything to suggest they were more than the typical patron getting their afternoon iced coffee and pastry fix.

Then she saw the familiar gray vehicle pull up to the curb, and her shoulders relaxed. She jumped up from her stool, leaving the empty coffee cup behind. She climbed into the front seat and Cruz took off. Raheem was in the back on his computer.

"Looks like everything went well," Shanice said.

"Very well. You did great." Cruz's eyes left the road for a

second. He placed a hand on her thigh, and her skin tingled. She wished she'd worn a skirt instead of the pants.

"Thank you. Maybe I could be a spy."

"Let's not get carried away," Raheem said before Cruz could even respond.

The three of them laughed.

"Tell me you found something," Cruz said. His gaze flicked up to watch Raheem in the rear-view mirror.

Raheem didn't respond right away, and Shanice turned in the seat to observe him. He was hunched over his computer and typing very fast.

"Found it. Precise, LLC is located in the Caymans." There were a few more taps on the keyboard. "Ladies and gentlemen, we now have the account numbers for every account Precise paid into. All twenty-two of them." He grinned at Shanice.

"Oh my goodness. We did it!" All she could think about was that they had managed to get the information and Dennis hadn't died in vain. Her excitement was short-lived when she saw Cruz's unsmiling face.

"We have a tail," he said.

"What?" Through the back window, Shanice saw a truck and a number of cars immediately behind them.

"Shit," Raheem said.

"Turn around and buckle up," Cruz said to Shanice.

Recalling how he had driven back in Miami, she did just that. Whatever he had planned, she needed to be ready for it. She snapped her seatbelt into place and gripped the handle on the car door.

She expected him to move quickly through the traffic, but instead he went with the flow, cruising along at a normal speed.

Shanice glanced at him. "Aren't you going to try to outrun them?" she asked.

"Too much traffic, so we have to lose them another way," Cruz explained. Tension radiated off his skin.

"Which car is it?"

"The blue Lincoln," Cruz answered.

Shanice checked the side mirror and saw the car in question. There were two men inside.

"Do you think it was my fault? Did I do something wrong?" She'd never forgive herself if she jeopardized everything they'd worked for today.

Cruz shook his head. "Could have been any of us, to be honest. Security guards caught us when we were in the accounting office. They could have called someone before we left the building."

He seemed calm, but she'd spent enough time with him to know his mind was going a million miles a second planning an escape route. Smooth and easy, he pulled onto the highway. The other car followed.

Minute after minute ticked by slowly, and the silence in the car shredded her nerves. She felt as if they were waiting for something but didn't know what. She didn't want to speak and break Cruz's concentration, but at the same time, she desperately wanted to understand what he was doing and how he intended to handle these people.

He was headed away from the motel, and she figured that was on purpose. Several times he switched lanes, and each time he did, the other car followed. Not right away, but after a while. That's when it dawned on her. He was checking their pace, determining how quickly they followed each time he moved.

She glanced over at him and he looked at her. His grim expression softened before he returned his gaze to the road ahead.

Accelerating slowly, Cruz pulled in front of an eighteen-wheeler. That kept them out of view of the blue Lincoln for several seconds, and then she saw them easing forward.

Cruz squeezed her knee, and the tension drained from her body. His unspoken message was simple—*I've got this.*

Suddenly, he took a hard left and swung the car onto the exit. Shanice braced her hand against the dashboard. Car tires squealed behind them, and she looked back to see the Lincoln had come to a halt in the middle of traffic. Horns blared at them and other car tires squealed as drivers fought not to hit each other.

One red Toyota was not so lucky. The car skidded and the owner swung the wheel to the right in an effort to avoid hitting the black sedan in front of him. He clipped the back fender of the sedan and a pickup crashed into him from behind.

During all of this commotion, a man jumped out of the Lincoln and ran to the railing. He pointed his gun at them and then dropped it in frustration, glaring as they followed the curve onto the road below.

Cruz floored the accelerator and weaved past traffic.

"We lost them," Shanice said, breathing easier.

"Not for long," Raheem said.

"He's right. They know what the car looks like, and they know what we look like. We can ditch this vehicle, but the best thing is to ditch Houston now that we have what we need."

The three of them remained quiet until Cruz pulled into the motel parking lot, and then they hurried up the stairs to their second-floor rooms.

Outside their door, Raheem handed Cruz a flash drive. "I copied the pertinent files. Here's everything you need."

He spoke with such finality, Shanice realized they were going to split up. The job was done. Although she'd only known Raheem for a short time, sadness came over her.

"As always, I appreciate your help." Cruz clapped him on the arm.

"Anytime." Raheem turned to Shanice and kissed the back of her hand. He flashed the same sexy grin he greeted her with the first time they met. "It was nice meeting you, Shanice.

Maybe we'll see each other again sometime." He glanced at Cruz, as if sending a message to him.

"It was nice meeting you, Raheem, and by the way, I'm a hugger."

She stepped into him and gave him a hug. He initially stiffened, but then he relaxed and hugged her back.

When they released each other, Raheem cleared his throat. "Take care."

He went down the hall, and she and Cruz entered their room.

"Pack what you need. Only what you *need*. Right now," Cruz said.

Shanice nodded and went to work.

WHILE SHE STUFFED items into her backpack, Cruz dialed Miles on his encrypted phone.

"Yes?"

"The job is done, and it's more complicated than we initially thought. You're not going to believe this. Cheng is going to want to know about it," he said, referring to the head of Plan B.

"Your assignment was off the books," Miles reminded him.

"And it should be on the books. A sitting senator of the United States is sending mercenaries after U.S. citizens, and he's killing cops." Cruz pulled across the heavy brown curtain and peered outside. He didn't see any unusual activity in the parking lot.

"*What?*"

"You heard me."

"You're sure about this?"

"No, but I'm certain of one thing—his buddy Randall Logan is involved, bribing police officers to intimidate and harass tenants in apartment complexes in five different states. He pays them a hefty sum, anywhere from five to six figures." He quickly went into the details they'd uncovered.

"So you have no proof Sandoval is involved, and even if you did, I'd have to kick this up the chain of command. We're talking about a goddamn sitting senator and the chairman of the Appropriations Committee. Plan B is not going to want to touch those allegations without proof. He has a lot of influence on how the money in the budget is allocated."

"Miles, my instincts tell me—"

"Cruz, I understand the gravity of what you're saying, but your instincts don't mean shit. You need proof. We can't go on a fishing expedition with Sandoval. Any investigation has to be handled delicately, carefully, and from what you've told me so far, I don't see the need for an investigation."

Cruz ran a weary hand down his face. He hated to admit it, but Miles was right. "I get it. I have a flash drive and other information that will bury Logan. I need to get it to you." Since this assignment was off the books, they hadn't established a secure channel to expedite the information to Miles.

"Where are you and how soon can you get here?"

"Houston, and I'm flying out tonight. We already picked up a tail. I'm ready to leave."

"Okay, by the time you land, I'll have everything sorted out."

"Be careful, Miles. Remember, I have a civilian with me."

"What about the senator's niece? Any indication that she's involved?"

"I can't confirm or deny, but my gut tells me she's not involved. I don't think she would have come to you if she was. It's him, Sandoval."

"You *think*." Miles sounded tired. "Send me a text as soon as you land. I'll send someone to pick you up from the airport."

"I don't trust anyone."

"Well, you'll have to trust me. Just get here, Cruz. I'll be waiting."

23

"Get in here!" Randall belted the words and then slammed down the phone. Resting an elbow on the chair's armrest, he rubbed his throbbing head with shaking fingers.

One minute later, his son Jacob entered the study.

Fuming, Randall demanded, "Why didn't you tell me they broke into the accounting office at Logan Towers today?"

His son looked very polished wearing a three-piece suit. Moments ago he'd come back from a meeting with investors, but Randall was not as interested in the results of the meeting as he was with the fiasco that had taken place at his company headquarters.

"I was handling it."

"Handling it? What exactly did you do to *handle* it?"

Jacob stiffened, an indication that he was biting his tongue, but he wouldn't dare talk back to Randall.

"Shanice Lawrence was spotted by Garrett, a member of our security team. He recognized her from the photo we'd given them when they'd broken into her apartment a couple of months ago. He called me and I told him to keep an eye on her.

She went into a Starbucks. He and another member of the team watched from nearby, intending to follow her to wherever she was headed, but unfortunately, she was picked up by two men. Our guys continued to follow them."

"*And...?*" Randall prompted impatiently.

His son smoothed a hand over his hair and mumbled something.

"What did you say?" Randall asked sharply.

"They got away."

Randall chuckled without amusement. "These people are running circles around us."

"She's obviously working with professionals," Jacob said defensively.

"I wish we were," Randall snapped.

Both men stared at each other before Jacob dropped his gaze.

Randall shoved angrily to his feet. Gripping his cane, he shuffled over to the window and gazed out at the landscape. Spread out before him were acres of land which he purchased with his own hard-earned money. He didn't care how other people defined "hard-earned." For him, that meant long hours in the office and using his sharp mind to one-up his opponents. It also meant sometimes he needed to bend the law so he could achieve his goals.

"What did they take from the accounting office?" he asked.

"The IT manager said they downloaded the accounting manager's entire computer," Jacob answered.

Randall's heart plummeted. Not good. "They know," he said in a deadpan voice.

"We can still stop them."

"How?" When his son didn't answer, he turned to face him. "Lucky for you, I have friends in high places. I happen to know that Miss Lawrence and her accomplice are headed to DC *tonight* to meet with the U.S. Attorney General. Put a team together and stop them."

"I want to be there, too."

"No. Absolutely not." Hand tightening on his cane, Randall shook his head vehemently. "You don't need to be that close. You get too close, you get your hands dirty."

Jacob stepped forward, his face hardening with resolve. "If I'm there, I can make sure they're successful. Let me do this for you, Dad."

Randall didn't like the idea of his son getting close to the action. All his life, he had kept his hands clean by hiring other people to do the dirty work. That allowed him to stay above the fray and sidestep the law on numerous occasions. If law enforcement had no real evidence, they couldn't tie him to any illegal activities.

But his son's earnest expression was his undoing. Though he didn't want Jacob to go to DC to handle that meddling woman and her friend, Jacob clearly wanted an opportunity to prove himself. With his military background, he might succeed.

"Take the jet. Get her, find out what she knows, and then kill her. But be careful. This man she's working with is clearly very dangerous and smart."

"I know who to call. They're former mercenaries and the best."

"Then go, and bring me some good news for a change."

24

Cruz sent a text as soon as they landed and confirmed that his supervisor, Miles, would send transportation for them.

Wary of their surroundings, Shanice stuck close to his side and kept her backpack wedged against her body as they walked through the airport. She'd wanted to nap on the flight but stayed awake the entire six and a half hours, unable to completely relax. Her only comfort on the journey from Houston was having Cruz in the seat beside her. He managed to sleep, and she envied his ability to disconnect and recharge.

He took her hand and gently squeezed her fingers. "It's going to be okay," he said quietly. "Remember what I told you? I won't let anything happen to you, and I meant that. Even if I have to come back from my grave to keep you safe."

"Not funny," Shanice said, bumping him with her hip. Though she wouldn't be surprised if he were able to keep her safe from the grave.

He smiled, and she relaxed. If he wasn't worried, she wouldn't be. He had the flash drive taped to his side under his shirt, and Shanice knew no one would be able to get their hands on it. They'd have to kill him first.

They didn't have long to wait outside before a black Chevrolet Suburban pulled up and a slender but wiry man jumped out from the passenger seat.

"How's it going?" he said with a grin.

He looked at Cruz when he spoke. With shaggy black hair and bright green eyes, he appeared young—probably no more than twenty.

"Great," Cruz said. "If I'd known Miles was sending you, I would have put in a request for someone else."

The young man chuckled and they shook hands and briefly embraced in a half hug.

"This is Shanice. Shanice, this is J.C."

"Nice to meet you," she said.

"Likewise."

They shook hands while Cruz placed their bags in the back of the vehicle.

"We're headed to the Department of Justice. Miles has arranged everything, including an escort." J.C. inclined his head at another black Suburban in the back containing three burly men.

They didn't acknowledge them. Their faces remained as expressionless as stone.

"Will Miles be there?" Cruz asked.

"Yes, sir."

They all climbed in, and Shanice greeted the driver. Where J.C. was rather young, the driver, who introduced himself as Sam, was older. He had a more seasoned appearance and an air of experience when he gave a curt nod in greeting.

When they pulled away from the curb, J.C. turned halfway in his seat and asked, "Where are you going after you talk to Miles and the U.S. Attorney General?"

"To sleep," Cruz answered.

"Where are you staying?"

"No idea yet."

J.C. obviously admired Cruz, but now that the initial friendly greeting had passed, Cruz was not as interested in conversation. He kept his eyes trained on their surroundings outside the vehicle.

As they cruised along, Shanice idly examined her hands. Wrinkling her nose at her chipped fingernails, she promised herself when this was all over, she'd treat herself to a mani-pedi. Maybe a massage, too. She sighed at the idea of a pampering session.

"How far away is the Department of Justice?" she asked.

"Only about five minutes away now," J.C. answered.

There wasn't much traffic this late at night, and Shanice wondered how long the short trip took during a normal work day.

They crossed the bridge that spanned the Potomac River, and her heart became heavy at the thought of her separation from Cruz. *What happens after the interview?* she wondered. Would he leave, like he said he would? Would she ever see him again? The conclusion to this mess didn't take as long as she'd expected. She thought they'd have more time together.

They slowed to a stop at a traffic light. The stately buildings signaled they were getting closer. This was her first time in DC and she considered spending a few days in town to do some sightseeing.

"Look out!"

Her head swung around at the sound of Cruz's voice, and she followed his line of sight to where a black Escalade had pulled across the road in front of them. A man hung out the window with an automatic rifle trained on them.

Sam slammed on the brakes. After that, everything happened fast.

Gunshots filled the air, and the few pedestrians in the street scattered like frightened mice.

The SUV tires flattened, shots coming from the Escalade in front and a black sedan parked on the side. The windshield shattered into pieces, and Shanice ducked as the ra-ta-tat-tat of gunfire from an assault rifle pummeled the steel doors.

Sam slumped over the wheel and the horn blared while the SUV, no longer under the control of its driver, coasted toward a parked mini-van.

"Ohmigod! Ohmigod, what is happening?" Shanice screamed.

But even as she asked, she acknowledged that was a ridiculous question. She knew exactly what was happening. They were being ambushed.

Cruz grabbed her wrist. "We have to—"

Boom!

The front of the Suburban upended, sending Shanice on the equivalent of a wild, crazy roller coaster ride. Ears ringing, she grappled at dead air in a vain attempt to set them back on their tires. The vehicle paused upright, as if deciding what to do, and then crashed onto its left side with flames shooting out of the engine.

Temporarily disoriented, Shanice shook her head to dispel the loud ringing in her ears. She was suspended by the seatbelt, which cut into her torso and neck.

Cruz fought with his stuck seatbelt. He cursed loudly. "Are you all right?" he asked.

Shanice barely heard him. He sounded muffled and far away. Still struggling to get her bearings, she opened her mouth to respond, but the words caught in her throat when her car door was yanked open and strong hands grabbed her by the neck.

Panicked, she choked out a cry. "Cruz!"

The man grabbed her under the arms and cut her seatbelt.

"Shanice!"

Cruz lunged as far as the seatbelt allowed. She reached for him and he grabbed her hand, but it wasn't enough. Her fingers slipped through his as she was hauled from the vehicle by two sets of hands.

"*Cruz!*" she screamed.

She did her best to struggle, determined not to get into the back of the car because she had no idea what her fate would be. She slammed her left elbow into the chest of the man beside her, and he retaliated with a stinging blow to the temple that made her see stars.

In essence, she was no match for the bigger men, and when one of them cocked a gun to the back of her head, she thought for sure she was dead.

"Get in the fucking car." He roughly shoved her in the back seat while the other man went around to the other side.

The driver pulled away immediately.

Shaking and terrified, Shanice cowered in the back, seated between the two men, both with dark hair. The one on the right had steely black eyes, but the one on the left—

Her breath caught. She recognized him from the photos in Dennis's box. He looked very much like Randall Logan, and when Raheem had done a quick internet search, they'd learned that he was Logan's youngest son, Jacob.

The one on her right spoke first. "You have something we want. If you want to live, you'll give it to us."

"I don't have anything."

"You sure about that?"

"Yes. The man you left behind in the Escalade has it. Not me."

Black Eyes sneered. "We'll see if you have the same answer when we get through with our thorough interrogation."

Jacob simply smiled, and Shanice's stomach dipped low with fear.

He had to get to her. Her wide, panicked eyes and ear-splitting scream would haunt him for the rest of his days if he didn't.

Cruz cut himself loose with a piece of broken glass and hoisted his body out of the capsized vehicle with a Sig Sauer P229 he lifted from the holster Sam had strapped to his side. Before he had exited, he spotted J.C.'s blood-spattered chest. He was about nineteen or twenty years old and was probably excited about being chosen for such an important mission. *Poor kid*, he thought, and cursed Miles and Plan B in his head.

The agency recruited its agents young, preferring people who came from damaged homes or who had no close family. There probably wouldn't be anyone mourning J.C.'s death.

As soon as Cruz landed on the ground, a shot pinged the undercarriage of the vehicle, and he took off running. The Escalade came barreling toward him. They must've stayed behind to make sure he was dead.

As more bullets whizzed by, he took a flying leap across the hood of an old station wagon, landing hard on his shoulder. Pain ripped up his neck, and he winced but managed to hold onto the gun.

With a quick glance to the right, he caught sight of the sedan carrying Shanice make a left down the street. *Goddammit.* He had to hurry if he planned to catch them.

The escort vehicle was in shambles, fire spewing from the engine and the sides dented with bullets. The occupants appeared to be dead. Like the Suburban he rode in, a bomb had detonated under it, and then the attackers had opened fire on the driver and the two passengers.

He heard the Escalade doors open and dropped to his stomach. Peering under the car, he saw two sets of feet moving stealthily toward him. Cruz aimed and fired twice, hitting both men in the ankle. They howled in pain and one collapsed to the ground.

He jumped up and fired two more shots from behind the vehicle, killing them and ducking when the man in the back seat pointed the AK-47 at him. A round of bullets rocked the car he used as a barricade, and Cruz crept toward the front and peeped over the hood.

The same man now had a bazooka on his shoulder.

Holy shit.

Cruz scrambled away, dropping into a roll behind a red sports car when the weapon hit the station wagon. He crouched into a ball, covering his head as the station wagon exploded and fragments of steel, rubber, and glass rained down around him.

Taking advantage of the carnage, Cruz circled around the front of the sports car. The man had no idea Cruz was no longer behind the torched vehicle. He crept to the other side of the Escalade, moving fast but staying low. He opened the back door, taking the enemy by surprise. The man swung toward him and Cruz shot him in the side of the head. He shot him a second time for good measure.

Assuming he started with thirteen rounds, he had seven left.

Cruz ran around to the other side, took hold of the man he shot, and dragged him out of the SUV. Then he hopped into the driver's seat and took off down a one-way street, flooring the accelerator.

25

The one-way street wasn't crowded, but one car veered out of the way, the driver angrily blaring his horn.

"*Lo siento*," Cruz muttered.

In his determination to catch up to Shanice and the kidnappers, he didn't have time to obey traffic laws. He only hoped he could find them before it was too late.

Driving like a bat out of hell, Cruz swung his gaze left to right, trying to quell the surging panic that he might not reach Shanice in time. He pulled onto another street, only certain they would be headed far away from Pennsylvania Avenue, but not certain which direction to go in.

Ahí está!

The sedan was ahead of him, driving at a normal pace so they wouldn't attract attention. They probably figured they were home free, too, but he had to stop them, and the only way he knew to do that meant risking harm to Shanice. Yet he had to take the chance.

Cruz rolled down the window. Pressing his foot on the gas, he came up behind the black sedan and took careful aim with the gun. His left hand wasn't his dominant hand, but he had to try. He focused and then fired a shot. The left tire popped and the car swagged to the right.

That slowed them down, but now they knew he was behind them. Shanice and the two men in the back seat turned around. Even from that distance he saw the fear in her eyes.

The man on the right poked his head out the window, hands gripping a rifle. Cruz steered the vehicle to the left and ducked. The shot went wide, missing the Escalade.

The driver accelerated, but with one tire shredded, they couldn't go very fast.

Cruz kept his eyes on the sedan. He wanted to take out the driver but couldn't risk hitting Shanice. They weren't exactly driving in a straight line.

The man on the left grabbed a handful of her hair and stuck the gun to her head. Cruz gripped the steering wheel with his empty hand. He'd get a lot of pleasure out of killing that guy. Gritting his teeth, he imagined putting a bullet in the man's head and watching his blood leak down onto his blue shirt.

Shots hit the front grill of the Escalade, and Cruz swung to the left out of the line of fire. Then the gunman made a mistake. He sat on the edge of the open window, turning himself into an easy target even as he leveled the gun at Cruz. Cruz swung into the right lane, and as his opponent lined up a shot, so did he.

Cruz squeezed once and missed. The man fired and he ducked, the bullet blasting through the seat behind him. That was way too close for comfort.

When the gunman focused on his car tire, Cruz knew that it was now or never. He fired again, aiming for center mass, and hit the man's shoulder. He grimaced and dropped the gun. Blood poured from the wound, and he moved to withdraw into the vehicle, but Cruz fired again, hitting him in the neck. His body slumped forward and fell out of the car.

Three bullets left.

"Come on, come on."

Blue Shirt to the left of Shanice scooted over in the seat, about to do the same as his friend. He rolled down the window, and Cruz lined up the next shot. He hit the back right tire and it exploded. The car shimmied and rocked and the left tire came off completely. Sparks shot from the bald wheel before it broke off and rolled away. The car wobbled some more, dragging on the road's surface until the driver rolled them to a stop on the side of the road.

Cruz slammed on the brakes. He didn't bother with throwing the SUV in park. It slowly rolled away as he raced toward the car. He leaped onto the trunk and ran up on the roof. As the driver climbed out, Cruz put a bullet in his head before he could turn all the way around.

Hearing movement to his right, he swung in that direction, arms extended, gripping the Sig Sauer. Shanice and the last gunman were out of the car. His eyes widened when he recognized the other man's face. Jacob, Randall Logan's son. He had his arm around Shanice's neck and the gun to her temple. Cruz loved that she was tall, but this was one time it worked against her because he couldn't get a clear shot with Jacob hiding behind her.

"Drop the weapon or I'll kill her," he growled.

"You kill her, and the next gun that goes off is mine. You'll get a bullet in the middle of your forehead."

"You're willing to risk her life?"

"You're willing to risk yours?" Cruz hopped off the roof, keeping the gun extended. "You okay, *mami*?" he asked.

"I-I'm scared," Shanice admitted.

"No need to be. I'm right here. Remember what I promised you?" His eyes flicked to hers briefly, and in that millisecond he saw naked terror. He would do whatever he could to make that expression go away.

"Y-yes. You said you wouldn't let anything happen to me."

"That's right. I keep my promises."

"Oh, isn't this sweet?" Jacob gritted his teeth as he spoke, eyes locked on Cruz. He pushed the barrel of the gun hard against Shanice's temple, and she winced and whimpered.

Cruz slowly circled them, his intention to get the other man's back to the vehicle, boxing him in and blocking any possible escape route.

"Remember that other thing I told you?" Cruz asked. "That thing that never happens?"

She was quiet, and then she replied, "Y-yes."

"You trust me, don't you?"

"Yes." That answer came out stronger and with more confidence.

"Good. Never, *mami*. Not once." He only had one bullet and had to make it count.

Time slowed as he waited, tense, ready for the next move. Her eyes filled with tears, and then she did exactly what he expected her to.

She jerked her head to the left.

Not a second later, Cruz fired off a round before her captor had a chance to react. The 9mm projectile hit him in the right eye and he fell backward, his arm still locked around Shanice.

They tumbled to the ground with Jacob falling on top of her.

She screamed and then yelled, "Get him off me! Get him off me!"

Cruz rushed over and dragged him off her. Sobbing, Shanice fell into his arms and buried her face in his neck. He squeezed her tight, doing his best to wipe the blood spatter from her arm and the right side of her face.

His shoulder ached, his body was bruised, but Shanice was safe.

"You're okay. You're okay," he whispered.

The sound of police sirens neared, and cruisers approached from opposite directions. One by one they stopped on squealing tires. Cruz and Shanice eased apart and squinted against the flashing lights as they were surrounded.

"Drop your weapon!" an officer yelled from behind his open car door.

All around them, police officers had their guns drawn. Six cruisers and twelve cops in all.

"Stay on your knees and don't make any sudden moves," Cruz whispered to Shanice.

Slowly, he placed his weapon on the ground and clasped his hands behind his head. Shanice followed suit.

He looked at her tear-streaked face, wishing he could pull her back into his arms and offer comfort. "It's going to be okay," he promised.

26

Shanice gingerly touched a hand to the tender spot beside her eyebrow. She had a headache and bruise from when Jacob had hit her after he and his accomplice yanked her from the SUV.

She could hear Miles and Cruz arguing behind the closed door. Either they didn't know she could hear them, or they didn't care. They'd been in there for ten minutes while she waited in the outer office.

The first five minutes she didn't hear a word, but then Cruz raised his voice and Miles responded by matching his tone.

"Bull. Shit," Cruz said.

"Shouldn't you be thanking me?"

Shanice appreciated Miles, even if Cruz didn't. She'd never been handcuffed before, and the police officers were none too gentle until two men, whom Cruz later explained had been sent by Miles, showed up at the police station as they were about to get booked. Cruz and Shanice were released within minutes.

"Thank you for what? I trusted you to get her here safely, and instead you almost got her killed!" Cruz yelled.

"*I* didn't almost get her killed. Somehow the information got leaked."

"On your watch. Who the hell leaked that we were coming, Miles?"

"I don't know yet. I'm working on it."

"You better damn well find out before I do."

"Lucky for you they didn't know who they were dealing with. They should have sent an army."

"Remind me to punch you in the face when this is all over."

Shanice couldn't believe Cruz was speaking to a supervisor that way. Then again, maybe she could.

"I'll be sure to do that," Miles said.

The door was yanked open and both men came out, faces set in angry lines. Miles wore a tan suit, and Cruz still had blood smeared all over him from holding her. Since their arrival, she had gone to the restroom and washed her face and cleaned up her hair as much as she could. She washed the blood off her arm, but her clothes were still stained with the sticky red stuff, and she couldn't wait to get naked and take a warm, cleansing shower.

Miles sat in the chair beside her, concern in his dark eyes. "How are you doing?" He was a good-looking man with dark skin, a full beard, and looked to be in his late thirties.

Before going into the office, Cruz had explained that Miles worked in a different building, but he'd arranged for the interview to take place at the U.S. Department of Justice because they would review the evidence and take over the investigation.

"I've been better," Shanice answered.

At least she still had her sense of humor. Either that or she'd crack under the strain of the night's events. Maybe she was getting stronger. Maybe she was in shock.

Miles smiled at her. "You've been through a lot, but the worst is over. Now we get to mete out justice. Here's what's going to happen. We're going to interview you and Cruz and get as much information as we can while the details are fresh in your memory. That's going to take several hours, and it's already late. I know we're asking a lot, but are you up to it?"

Shanice glanced at Cruz, who stood like a hulking sentinel standing guard over the conversation. She had no doubt if she said she wasn't up to the interview, he'd whisk her out of there and there was nothing Miles or anyone else could do about it.

Returning her attention to Miles, she said, "I'm ready to do whatever it takes, even if it means staying here all night."

A smile lit up Miles's face. "That's exactly what I wanted to hear. There's one more thing you should know. I told Cruz that we can't do anything about Senator Sandoval, but we can make sure we nail Logan."

That part of the conversation must have taken place before they started yelling.

"Does that mean Senator Sandoval will get away with his involvement with Logan Investors?" Shanice asked.

"Assuming he's privy to what took place, I'm afraid so. The truth is, we don't have enough to pursue an investigation, and we think it's best not to implicate him at all."

Shanice didn't like that resolution, and by the grim set to Cruz's lips, he didn't, either. But she had to believe that Miles and the Department of Justice knew what they were doing.

They left the office and went down a long hallway into a more opulent room that contained a gold and burgundy rug that covered most of the floor. Portraits of past Attorneys General hung on the wood-paneled walls, and the United States and the districts' flags sat erect in front of a long conference table.

There were three other men in the room. One sat before a stenotype, while the other two were dressed in suits and stood when Shanice, Cruz, and Miles entered.

The older man with gray hair approached and extended his hand to Shanice. "Miss Lawrence, I'm U.S. Attorney General

George Callahan. Your interview will be video recorded, and we'll also have someone taking notes."

Shanice nodded. "Okay."

The other man extended his hand. "I'm Michael Monroe, with Senator Sandoval's office. Because of the close relationship Senator Sandoval had with Dennis Ray, he wanted to be kept abreast of what happens here tonight. I'm only here to observe and report back to him."

Shanice glanced at Cruz, whose right hand clenched at his side, but he said nothing.

"Nice to meet you," Shanice said.

Both men reclaimed their seats. Shanice sat down and Cruz sat beside her. He took her hand under the table and squeezed. He didn't look at her, but his touch made all the difference. She almost burst into tears at the gentle, comforting pressure. Having him by her side made her feel stronger and not so alone.

"Are you ready to get started?" Miles asked, seated across from them.

"Yes," Shanice replied.

The other men nodded, and Miles pressed a button on a control box in the middle of the table. A flashing light caught her eye in the front wall. That's when she noticed the video camera lens. The recording had started.

Miles began. "For the record, my name is Miles Garrison. The date and time is..."

IN THE BACKSEAT of a limousine provided by Miles, Shanice sat with her eyes closed, the back of her head resting against the seat. She no longer cared to see the sights. It was almost dawn and all she wanted was to crawl into bed and get a good night's sleep. The way she felt—battered and weary—she was pretty sure she wouldn't wake up until the next day.

They arrived at a hotel that would be a splurge if she were to pay for it herself. A chandelier sparkled in the ceiling, and white marble tile spanned from the reception desk to the carpeted sitting area.

A smiling female employee greeted them at the door. The statuesque woman wore a crisp blue uniform and her dark hair was pulled into a bun.

Shanice couldn't help being a little jealous of her clean clothes and neat hair.

"Hello, I'm Stella. We have your rooms ready. Follow me, please."

Shanice trudged behind the hotel employee with Cruz pulling up the rear. They rode the elevator in silence and exited on the fifth floor.

"Your rooms are next door to each other," the woman explained.

She opened the first one, and Shanice entered. Her backpack was already in there, having been retrieved from the scene where the Suburban had been overturned. She thought about J.C. and Sam and the other men in the escort vehicle. Like Dennis, their lives had been taken to hide the misdeeds of an evil, greedy man.

"Is it to your liking?" Stella asked.

The tastefully decorated room was designed in creams and whites and contained a king bed with big fluffy pillows, a sofa, and a desk and chair.

"Yes. Thank you."

"Sir, will you follow me please?"

"Good night, Cruz," Shanice said.

He hesitated, eyes lingering on her. "Good night."

Shanice closed the door and leaned against it.

They hadn't said much since they left the Department of

Justice, and she wondered what his plans were. If he didn't leave the city right away, maybe they could have one more meal together before they went their separate ways.

With an aching heart, Shanice went into the bathroom. A humongous tub awaited her, as well as all manner of bath salts and bath gels. Everything she could want for a relaxing escape. But as much as she wanted to languish in a warm bath, she settled for a shower and washed her hair and face, wincing when she accidentally irritated the bruise on her temple.

She shoved her feet into slippers that matched the hotel robe and went into the bedroom. She double-checked that the door was locked and the safety latch was on. So much had happened in the past two days—had it really only been *two days*?—she didn't know when she'd feel completely safe again.

She took an ibuprofen for her ever-present headache and removed a bottle of water and a small box of herb crackers from the mini fridge and settled on the bed. She should go to sleep, but her mind couldn't rest. She couldn't stop thinking about Cruz next door. Was he asleep yet?

Her question was answered when a knock sounded on the door that connected her room to his. Shanice jumped up and unlocked it.

"*Hola*," he said.

"*Hola*," she said.

Cruz was barefoot and wearing one of the hotel robes, too. His face broke into a crooked smile that made her heart twist in her chest.

"Want some company?"

"I would love some company."

They closed the door and without another word disrobed and climbed into the bed together, both of them naked. Under normal circumstances, she'd want to have sex, but her libido was hiding behind a curtain of weariness. Cruz must have been having the same experience, because he simply lay on his back and held her. It was the best feeling to simply lie next to him. That not-so-safe feeling disappeared in his strong arms.

"It'll be daylight soon," he remarked.

"Yeah." Shanice trailed a finger down his left pec.

"The DOJ is sending investigators after Logan and the police officers. Miles is confident the officers will implicate Logan as soon as they find out he's been knocking them off to cover his tracks."

"He did that because of what Dennis discovered," she said.

"Yes. Tying up loose ends, so to speak."

"Do you really think Senator Sandoval is involved?"

"Yes."

"Do you think he'll get away with it?"

"He already has."

His answer saddened her. "He'll never see justice."

"Sometimes justice doesn't come through normal channels."

It was probably better she didn't know what he meant by that.

"When do you leave?" Shanice asked. The question caused a strain on her heart.

"I'm not sure. I don't have any pressing engagements right now. You?"

"I don't know. But when I do, I want to go somewhere quiet and peaceful, I guess."

"That makes sense. You've been through a lot."

His heart beat steadily under her cheek as his fingers slowly trailed up and down the arm she had thrown across his chest. Suddenly, he stopped moving, and she lay there in silence, holding still, waiting for him to say more.

"Come with me, Shanice."

She lifted her head, not sure she'd heard him correctly. Their eyes locked.

"Where?" she whispered.

"I have a house in Islamorada in the Florida Keys. It's quiet and peaceful and right on the water." He tenderly smoothed a hand over her hair and tucked a curl behind her ear.

"Sounds heavenly."

"Then you'll come?"

Her heart melted. She still didn't know his last name, and relationships were complex enough without secrets and half-truths muddying the waters. But none of that mattered. She wanted to be with him and gave the only answer that made sense.

"Yes."

"I disappear for weeks at a time, sometimes months—and I can't tell you where I'm going. One day, I might not come back. Are you sure you can handle that? A life of not knowing if you'll ever see your man again?"

Her heart hurt at the possibility of harm coming to him, that one day he might never come back to her. "No, I'm not sure, but I want to be with you. I'll make the sacrifice. You can't talk me out of coming with you, Cruz. My answer is still yes."

27

Randall watched as FBI agents carted computers and boxes of documents from his office. The yellow letters on their blue jackets were an ugly, glaring indictment as they carried out their duties on a weekday, in full view of staff and a barrage of onlookers in the street.

"Mr. Logan?" A female agent with her red hair in a ponytail stood beside his chair. "I need you to come with me, sir." A pair of handcuffs dangled from her hand.

"Is that really necessary? I'm an old man, and I need my cane."

He eased from the chair and she stepped aside. Using his cane, Randall walked with as much dignity as he could muster. He exited the office to the stares of his assistant and a few employees that had gathered in the outer office. Randall kept his eyes trained straight ahead, focused on nothing but the air in front of him.

His life was a wreck. The ensuing investigation would tarnish his name and destroy the empire he had built over the last forty years.

His youngest son had been murdered. Pain bloomed in his

chest at the thought of Jacob being shot down in the street like an animal. His boy, his successor, the one who inspired his greatest sense of pride—was gone for good. His oldest son, the traitor, had turned against him and was working with the FBI. Joseph, his longtime friend, was no longer taking his calls.

Randall stood in front of the closed elevator doors with an agent on either side of him.

This type of upheaval late in life could kill a weaker man, but Randall Logan was strong. He might be down, but he wasn't out, and he had plenty to live for.

Not the least of which was revenge.

28

"Hey, Mr. Hudson!" Shanice waved to the neighbor, who owned a small bookstore and coffee shop on the island.

"Hey there!" Seated on his porch, the older man's tanned, wrinkled face broke into a grin as he waved back.

Shanice parked her bike in the cobblestone driveway of Cruz's house and let herself in the front door, balancing a bag of groceries on her hip.

Islamorada was a village on six islands in the Keys. Known as the "Sportfishing Capital of the World," its tranquility was exactly what she had been hoping for after the chaotic period in her life. Since coming there, she'd stayed busy visiting the diving museum, hanging at Hudson's Bookstore, and taking an ecotour.

Shanice walked across the bamboo floors, past the dining room and into the living room where a large window looked out at the back yard and the Gulf beyond. Cruz's three-bedroom house was an open floorplan that sat on a lot he'd purchased years ago in a small exclusive neighborhood. Working with a builder, he'd designed the mostly white interior and the exterior, which included a swimming pool and hot tub that could be accessed by walking down the stairs from the covered deck into the back yard. The boat slip allowed them to jump in his small boat and island-hop at their convenience.

She'd spoken to Beatrice a couple of times in the past two weeks. The older woman assured her that she didn't blame her for what happened and was glad that she was finally safe. She spoke to Ava once, giving her limited information about her pursuit of justice for her dead friend, and her run from killers. She did let Ava know she'd met someone but didn't tell her it was their favorite customer. She wanted to keep that to herself a little bit longer.

She talked to her mother almost every day, including this morning. She'd flown to Arizona to spend time with her but returned after a few days because she missed the love bubble she and Cruz were enclosed in.

Shanice put away the groceries and then prepared two glasses of iced lemonade before padding to the back deck that overlooked the pool and hot tub. She took a seat in one of the chairs and waited for Cruz to notice she was back.

He was swimming laps, and when he saw her, he pulled himself out of the pool, wearing only a navy-blue Speedo, water dripping down his muscular body.

"Brought you something," Shanice said, holding up one of the glasses.

He leaned down and gave her a quick kiss. His firm, moist lips never failed to make her tingle.

"I think you're enjoying your time off," she said.

"I am. Because I have good company." He took the glass and sat down across from her.

Shanice picked up the book he had been reading earlier —*The Great Influenza: The Story of the Deadliest Pandemic in History.*

"How is this?" she asked, flipping to the bookmarked page where he'd stopped.

"Fascinating. I can barely put it down. I think you'll want to read it when I'm done."

Shanice flipped to the first page. "If you like it that much, I'll definitely have to check it out."

The phone on the table beside her rang.

"It's a video call, from Raheem," she said, handing it to him.

Cruz answered the call. "*¿Que bola, acere?* Is that a beach I see? Don't tell me you're back in Rio."

His friend laughed. "Of course. I might move here permanently and make this my base."

"You have a woman down there, don't you?"

"Wom*en*," Raheem corrected with a laugh.

Shanice smiled and shook her head.

"As much time as you spend there, shouldn't you be fluent in Portuguese now?"

"You know I'm no good at languages—except the language of love."

Shanice couldn't see the wolfish grin spread across his face, but she heard it.

Cruz groaned. "*Dios*, that was really bad, *acere*."

Raheem laughed. "Enough about me. How's life in the slow lane?"

"So far so good."

Shanice went to stand over Cruz's shoulder. "Hi." She waved at Raheem.

"You both look happy, so I guess everything is going well. I was just checking on you."

"We're doing fine." Shanice rested a hand on Cruz's wet shoulder.

"I've been keeping up with the news and saw what happened to Logan. Couldn't have happened to a better guy."

The FBI seized his records and forensic accountants were in

the process of digging into his financials, where they expected to find tax avoidance and other illegal activities. He'd already been charged with six counts of murder in the case of the dead police officers. The others, after learning that he was killing them off to tie up loose ends, agreed to testify against him regarding his scheme to force tenants out of their homes.

"And Dennis's name has been cleared," Shanice said.

The *Houston Times* did an entire series of articles about Dennis and his investigative work and had interviewed her for the series. From what she understood, they'd tried to interview his wife, too, but Karen had declined the invitation. Instead, she sent a heartfelt letter of gratitude to Cruz and Shanice through Miles, thanking them for clearing her husband's name. Their last contact with her was when she paid the balance of Cruz's fee.

"No word on the senator's involvement?" Raheem asked, a frown of concern marring his forehead.

"Nothing's going to come of it. Miles refuses to touch it," Cruz said, sounding irritated.

"I don't blame him. Ruffle the wrong feathers, and the next thing you know, they'll shut down the agency."

Cruz nodded, oddly reticent in his response.

"Shanice, make sure he continues to take care of himself. He works too hard."

"I will," she said with a grin. "You take care of yourself, too."

"I will." Raheem threw up the peace sign and hung up.

Cruz pulled her down onto his lap, and she draped her arms around his shoulders. "I had a great idea today."

"What?"

"No cooking for you tonight. I'm taking you to Key West for dinner, dancing, and we can spend the night at a local hotel and come back in the morning. How does that sound?"

"Sounds *ah*-mazing," Shanice replied. "I can't wait."

SUNLIGHT STREAMED in through the windows of the house and shone a spotlight on their lovemaking. The sound of rain hitting the roof made their lazy morning tryst that much more intimate.

Cruz dragged Shanice to the edge of the bed and set her ankles on his shoulders. His downstroke was powerful and hit deep. He made her take all of him, filling her core with such pleasure her entire being trembled with each dominant stroke. He forced the pleasure on her and tore the air from her lungs as his body constantly sliced into hers.

The heat from the early morning sex act made Shanice's skin damp as she reveled in every thrust of his hips between her thighs. Gripping his muscular arms, she arched higher to take more of him.

She moaned, begged, pleaded, and looped one arm around his neck so that she could drag him closer and sink her teeth into his strong throat. Sex was always like this with him. Rough, even when it was tender. Strong, intense, from the very first moment they made love. The night she locked eyes with this virile, sexy man in The Bookish Attic, she'd been thrown for a loop. Her unsteadiness only increased in the three weeks since she moved into his house in the Keys.

He groaned, forging his body deeper into hers. She met each thrust by gripping his deltoids, tightening around his erection until she came undone. An orgasm rippled through her loins up into her belly, and she cried out, tightening her legs around his neck. Seconds later, he let out a low groan and collapsed on top of her. He was certainly not light, but the weight of him was comforting and reassuring.

Rolling onto his back, Cruz let out a heavy breath and stared up at the ceiling.

"Good morning," he said.

Shanice giggled, twisting onto her side and looking at his profile. "Dare I say it? I love this new way of waking up in the morning."

He shifted onto his side and faced her, too. "Well, that's perfect then. Because I was thinking this should be the way we start every morning."

He was too much. With the sexy Cuban accent, intense umber eyes, and a warm smile that brightened her day whenever she saw it, she couldn't have asked for a better man.

She stroked his hair-roughened jaw. He hadn't shaved in over a week. "I like the beard," she said.

"¿Sí?" He rolled on top of her and nuzzled her neck.

"Yes." Shanice let out a peal of laughter, twisting in his arms as he tickled her. "Behave."

She slapped away his hand and pushed him off.

"I'm hungry. You hungry?"

"Mhmm." He folded his arms behind his head and watched her get dressed.

Shanice buttoned her white shirt. "What do you want for breakfast?"

"Is there any more fruit salad left?"

"Yep. Fruit salad, bacon, and waffles?"

"That sounds good. Now I'm extra hungry." He rubbed his bare belly.

"Then I better hurry up and feed you." Shanice pulled on a pair of shorts and then leaned down to give him a quick smack on the lips. "Breakfast coming right up, my dear."

29

Shanice knew the moment his warm body rolled away from hers.

She'd gotten used to spending time with Cruz, used to his presence. She'd woken up almost as soon as he left the bed with the phone glued to his ear.

He walked naked to the patio door, the sunlight streaming through the sheer drapes illuminating his tawny-colored skin and highlighting the lines of his muscular body and the scars that disclosed the harshness of his chosen profession. He didn't say much, and the conversation didn't last long. Maybe only two minutes. But afterward, he dropped his head and stared at the phone.

"What is it?" she asked quietly, sitting up in the bed.

Cruz turned to her and smiled, but she could see that he was troubled.

"That was Miles. They have a job for me. This one is out of the country."

She'd known this day would come but hoped they had more time.

He climbed into the bed as the dull ache of regret pushed

tears to the corners of her eyes. Their time together hadn't been very long. Barely a month, but only if you counted the days when they were running for their lives.

"I understand," she said.

His hand cupped her cheek, and his thumb gently brushed the corner of her mouth.

"I want this to be the last one," he said.

Shanice held his hand and kissed the middle of his palm. Shaking her head, she said, "You don't mean that."

"I've been thinking about leaving the agency, and it's the only thing that makes sense. What I do is dangerous work, and I don't want you to worry or get tangled up in my missions."

"You'll miss the adventure. You'll get bored."

Cruz shrugged. "I'll adjust."

"Can you? You've worked for the government almost half your life, and you're very good at what you do. This work is in your blood." She wanted him to stop, but not if it meant his happiness.

"Something else is in my blood now. You."

Shanice cupped his face, bringing her lips close to his. "Can I tell you something?"

"Sure. Anything."

She swallowed hard. "I love you."

He smiled his crooked grin. "I love you, too."

She smiled back, her heart beating faster with elation. She used to think you couldn't really know someone or love them until you'd spent a lot of time with them. Her last relationship had been a bust even though she'd known her boyfriend for years. But the truth was, until now, she'd never known what real love could be.

Cruz had given her a new perspective. In a short time, he'd taught her there was no timeline where love was concerned. Words like "the norm" were irrelevant when it came to matters of the heart. She'd fallen in love with him and already couldn't imagine her life without him in it.

How did this happen? How did she fall so hard for a man she'd known only a short time, with no reservations that he was her soulmate—the one made for her?

"And you're sure you want to walk away from your career?" Shanice asked in a soft voice.

"I've never been surer of anything in my life. You're my future, Shanice. Maybe I'll start that security company I told you about. Or I'll do something else. Whatever I decide, I want you beside me."

She kissed him, their lips melting together in a soft, affectionate caress. Sliding a leg between his thighs, she pushed him onto his back and settled on top of his chest.

Cruz smoothed his hands down the curve of her back and let them rest on her butt cheeks. He squeezed and lifted his pelvis into hers, groaning as he did so.

"When do you leave?" Shanice asked.

"Tomorrow."

God, she would miss him. Everything about him. The earthy, citrusy tang of his cologne, his deep laughter, and the way he touched her as if he never wanted to stop.

Shanice swallowed the pain of disappointment and said a quick prayer for his safe return. "Then let's make the most of the time you have left."

Cruz had never been so reluctant to leave on assignment before, but as he kissed Shanice goodbye at the door, her eyes filled with concern, he badly wished that he had a choice.

He'd only seen his life the way it had always been—alone. But Shanice had him thinking about lifestyle changes he'd never considered before—like home. Family. Love. He wished that he had a regular job, one where he left in the morning and came back in the evening to this woman who had turned his house into a home.

"Please be safe," she whispered, standing on tiptoe and gripping his shirt in her fists.

"It's nice to have someone so concerned about me. I think I could get used to this." Cruz dropped one last kiss to her lips and got in one more squeeze of her delectable bottom before he pulled back. "I have to go before I miss my flight," he said with regret.

"Okay. Take care."

He walked to the car and tossed in his duffel bag. The agency expected him to be gone at least two months, but he intended to cut that time short by a significant amount.

He waved to her at the door. She stood in a short silk robe, head resting against the frame. His future, and the more he thought about it, his wife. He was going to marry Shanice Lawrence, and he would do so as soon as he came back.

Shanice blew him a kiss as he backed out of the drive, and he drove off to the airport with a heavy heart.

Once there, he picked up his new identity in a locker and used it to get through security. On the plane, he fired off a quick text to Shanice and then settled in for the flight to DC and his briefing with Miles. A trip to DC wasn't always necessary, but this particular mission required the stop before he flew to Europe where he'd pose as a gun smuggler.

When the plane landed, he read Shanice's text and sent another one to her before climbing into the car that had been sent for him. The trip didn't take long, and soon he was walking down the cold hallway with a white tiled floor and white walls made of cement that were several feet thick.

The Plan B offices were underground, as secretive in location as the organization itself. At the outer door, Cruz placed his eye to a biometric lens and the door opened with a click, allowing him to enter. The environment changed drastically on the inside. There were warm colors, carpet, and large comfy chairs made up for the lack of natural light. The man seated at the front desk nodded at him.

"You can go in. He's waiting for you."

Not breaking stride, Cruz strolled into Miles's inner office. Miles was standing in front of a painting, hands clasped behind his back. He turned slowly to face Cruz.

"Good to see you," he said. "Let's get started."

The conversation took approximately thirty minutes, and Miles handed him documents and other materials he'd need for the trip. At the end, Cruz had a better understanding of what he was expected to do, how long the mission was expected to take, and if he would have any partners while overseas.

When they finished, he didn't move.

"Do you have any news about who leaked that Shanice and I were coming to DC?"

"It was J.C.," Miles said with a regretful shake of his head.

Miles's answer was completely unexpected. "Son of a...and he got himself killed in the process. Who did he tell?"

"That I don't know. We're still digging around trying to get the details about his contact without tipping anyone off. That's all I know for now."

"I want a name, Miles," Cruz said in a hard tone, barely keeping his temper in check.

"I know you do. So do I. I'm working on it. You have any more questions?" Miles clasped his hands on the desk.

"No, but I need to talk to you."

"About what?"

"This is hard for me to say, but I put a lot of thought into my decision. This will be my last mission, Miles. I'm retiring from Plan B."

Miles busted out laughing as if he had said something

outrageously funny. When Cruz didn't join him in laughing, he sobered and stared at him in disbelief.

"You're serious? This is your life. You've been a part of Plan B since you were eighteen years old."

Cruz shrugged. "It's no longer enough. I want a real life, a family." All these years he'd been a lone wolf. Shanice could change that.

Miles snorted. "Believe me, that's not all it's cracked up to be."

"But you have that—a family—and I don't."

"You can have both," Miles said.

Cruz shook his head. "I don't want both."

"You're just going to walk away from the agency?" Miles shook his head. "No way. You can't resign. You're too good, and your country needs you. You're only thirty years old and have a lot of years left to work."

"I've worked for my country for twelve years. That's plenty. I can start a business. Or simply take time off and figure out what I want to do." The conversation with Shanice had really cemented in his mind the idea of starting a security firm. It could be another outlet for him.

Miles laughed. "Look. Take some time to think about your decision. Don't be hasty. If you want more time off, I'll see what I can do."

"I'm supposed to believe you have my back? You didn't have my back when I asked you for an escort from the airport on the Logan thing."

Miles's eyes flashed angrily. He didn't like being called out on his failure. "That came from higher up the chain. You know that. Had I been allowed to handle things my own way, no one would have discovered your schedule and the ambush would have never taken place."

"Then let the higher ups know I'm done. My mind is made

up. Let them know, Miles. When I get back, I'm retiring after I'm debriefed."

"Cheng won't be happy."

"Cheng can kiss my Cuban ass."

Miles tapped his thumb on the arm of the chair. "Wow, I never thought I'd see the day."

Cruz stood, feeling as if a ton of granite had been lifted off his back. "I'll see you when I get back."

Miles studied him, disbelief evident in his eyes. Cruz had really shocked him with his decision.

"Sure. I'll see you when you get back."

30

F lowers. Check.

Engagement ring. Check.

Cruz flexed his fingers on the steering wheel, nervous in a way he couldn't remember ever being before. He could stare down the barrel of a gun and travel around the world fighting enemies of his country—evil people who thought nothing of taking his life and the lives of others. Yet his palms were sweating at the thought of asking the woman he loved for her hand in marriage.

Until now, he never thought he would be in this position, anxious to get married and start a family. But Shanice changed his mind, and he wanted to get married and start a family with her. He only hoped that she wanted to do those things with him.

Since his return to Florida, he had tried to reach her, but her phone had gone straight to voicemail. She could be at Hudson's Bookstore, one of her favorite hangouts on the island, or simply busy. Whatever she was doing, he was anxious to see her, anxious to give her a big kiss after six weeks apart.

His phone beeped and he glanced at the screen. Finally, she had responded.

Sorry I missed your call. I'm at home now. Where are you?

Two minutes away. Can't wait to see you.

She sent him a series of hearts and he grinned. Darn, he couldn't wait to grab her in his arms.

Cruz turned down the street toward his house, and a navy-blue two-door car rolled by him, the tinted windows so dark he couldn't see the interior or who was driving. He'd never seen this car before in their little neighborhood. Instinctively, he glanced at the back of the vehicle in his side view mirror and committed the license plate to memory.

When his house came into view, his heart thumped faster because he was excited to see Shanice again. He'd been unable to contact her while overseas, but sent a single postcard after three weeks. It didn't contain any identifying information, but he'd wanted her to know he was all right. The past six weeks had been the longest of his life, but knowing she'd been waiting here for him had made the wait easier.

Boom!

Cruz slammed on the brakes as his house exploded before his eyes. Glass, brick, and pieces of wood burst into the sky and rained down into the yard and onto the surrounding properties. Shocked, he stared at his demolished home.

What the hell?

Shaking out of his daze, he dialed Shanice's number. No answer. He tossed aside the phone and stumbled out of the vehicle, leaving it in the middle of the street as he raced toward the burning building. Near the flames, the intense heat seared his skin and he staggered back. Cruz stared at the carnage, coughing as smoke and ash filled the air.

Dear God, she couldn't be inside. *Please.* No.

He looked at the message she'd sent.

I'm at home now.

Two of his neighbors came running out onto the street, one of them holding up a phone to film while the other called 911.

Not much was left of the building. Whatever explosive device they had used had been very effective.

"Shanice," he whispered. The tightness in his chest gripped his entire body.

Maybe she wasn't really at home. Maybe she was in the back yard and safe. Maybe, just maybe this wasn't happening. Maybe he was still on the plane and needed to wake up.

But minutes later, he had to accept that this was not a dream. This was his reality, and all the plans he'd made went up in flames like his house. Shanice was nowhere to be found.

He watched firefighters douse what was left of the burning building with gallons of gushing water. Mr. Hudson called his name, but he didn't react. All he could do was stare.

Finally, it hit him. He would never see Shanice again. He would never hold her again.

"Shanice," he whispered, voice trembling.

His body became weak, puttylike. He dropped to his knees on the hard street as pain ripped through him. Tears blurred his eyes and burned his nose. Fingers clenched, he let out a roar like a wounded animal—so deep, so raw, so pained, that everyone who heard him turned and stared.

THE WALK to Nancy Cheng's office seemed long. Cruz's legs and feet felt as if they had been encased in cement, but that was because he'd barely slept in three days and could only remember eating once during the same period.

Nancy asked for a meeting with him to discuss his decision to leave. He'd only met her once, and that had been at an event when she took over as the new director—a low-key function at a DC hotel, labeled a wedding reception or some such nonsense to keep it under the radar and not let word get out that half the people in attendance were spooks working for a secret government organization.

As Cruz waited in the outer office, he was more convinced than ever he'd made the right decision to leave Plan B. There was no doubt in his mind that whoever killed Shanice had done so to hurt him. His work had caught up with him, and the perpetrator could have been from an assignment from years ago, or as recently as his work against Peaslee or Logan. They'd used high-level explosives, maximizing the damage and making what was left of her body unrecognizable. She'd simply been collateral damage, and he had a hard time accepting that she'd lost her life because of him.

Nancy looked up from behind a heavy oak desk when he entered. She didn't smile and neither did Cruz.

"You wanted to see me?"

"Yes, I did. Have a seat, please."

She was dressed in a designer pantsuit and wore a simple gold necklace around her neck. It was hard to tell exactly how old she was, but he figured her to be in her early fifties at least. No one got into the position of director without earning their stripes in the trenches. Legend had it, Nancy had at one time been a deadly agent in the field, working strictly as an assassin to take out anyone who posed an overt threat to CIA operations overseas.

Cruz sat in the chair in front of her desk.

Nancy leaned back in her chair. "Miles told me that you want to leave us. I didn't believe him. I assumed he'd misunderstood, so I thought I'd speak directly to you myself. If you need a break, you can have one, Cruz. If you need more money, name your price." Her smooth voice carried the accent of someone from the Midwest.

"I don't need a break, and I don't need more money. I simply can't do this anymore. My debt to the agency has been paid, and I'm done with Plan B for good."

He'd spent the past three days in a foggy shell of numbness he still hadn't managed to fully extricate himself from. Nothing seemed real. The world had turned gray, and the light Shanice had brought into it had been completely snuffed out.

Nancy smiled slightly. "You can't quit the organization, Cruz. You're too good at what you do. We need you."

If she thought she could talk him out of his decision, she had another think coming. Nothing would change his mind.

"I'm ready to do something else."

Nancy tossed the pen she'd been holding onto the desk. "What are you going to do? Take up knitting?"

"I'll think of something."

"Where is this coming from, Cruz? Is this because of your girlfriend, the one you met on that off-the-books job you took in Miami?"

"Yes. She's the main reason."

"Isn't she dead?"

She asked the question so carelessly, the words cut through him like an extra-sharp machete. He flinched at the pain that wouldn't be assuaged any time soon.

"Yes, she's dead."

"Then why are you leaving?"

"Because I want to."

"You're an assassin, a spook, a government agent. Am I supposed to believe you're simply going to settle down and live an ordinary life in the suburbs?" She scoffed at the idea. "A leopard never changes its spots."

"That's where you're wrong. Nothing can keep me with the agency, and now that the woman I love is gone, there's less incentive for me to stay. I have to live my life, and that's what I intend to do."

He stood and walked to the door.

"How? What does a man with your high IQ do now? Your file lists you as prone to violence. Do you really think you could live a normal life? Don't be ridiculous. Continue to work for change, in her memory."

He stopped at the door. "If you knew anything about Shanice, you'd know she wanted me to do what made me happy. *In her memory*, I'm going to do just that."

He walked out the door and minutes later was driving away. The guilt would never leave him, knowing that he caused Shanice's death. One thing was for certain, he would not rest until he found out who killed her.

And he would make them pay.

ALSO BY DELANEY DIAMOND

Coming in March 2021

Until Death (Plan B #2)

Years later, Cruz Cordoba is back!

In the exciting conclusion to Cruz and Shanice's love story, he's ready to handle more bad guys and has assembled a team to help him do it.

Free short stories available at www.delaneydiamond.com.

ABOUT THE AUTHOR

Delaney Diamond is the USA Today Bestselling Author of sweet, sensual, passionate romance novels. Originally from the U.S. Virgin Islands, she now lives in Atlanta, Georgia. She reads romance novels, mysteries, thrillers, and a fair amount of nonfiction. When she's not busy reading or writing, she's in the kitchen trying out new recipes, dining at one of her favorite restaurants, or traveling to an interesting locale.

Enjoy free reads and the first chapter of all her novels on her website. Join her mailing list to get sneak peeks, notices of sale prices, and find out about new releases.

Join her mailing list
www.delaneydiamond.com

facebook.com/DelaneyDiamond
twitter.com/DelaneyDiamond
instagram.com/authordelaneydiamond
bookbub.com/authors/delaney-diamond
pinterest.com/delaneydiamond

Made in the USA
Columbia, SC
02 December 2020